SAVING HOPE

LIESE SHERWOOD-FABRE

AWARD-WINNING AUTHOR AND
PUSHCART PRIZE NOMINEE

Praise for *Saving Hope*

"An alpha female heroine and a tantalizing premise that toys with the most basic of emotions — a parent's drive to save their child. Nothing frilly or fancy, just good old-fashioned, gimmick-free storytelling. And what could be better than that."

— Steve Berry, New York Times' bestselling author of the Cotton Malone series and The Romanov Prophecy.

"Liese Sherwood-Fabre has concocted an extremely well-written story that grabs you from the beginning and holds you relentlessly through all the twists and turns until the unexpected end."

— Paula G. Paul, winner of the Willa award.

In loving memory of
Nancy Jones Castilla, PhD.
Teacher, mentor, friend.

Table of Contents

Chapter One

Siberia, 2000

Alexandra Pavlova jolted upright, her maternal senses snapping to alert. The garlic she'd placed about the room tinged each breath and settled on her tongue. For two days, she'd spoon-fed the girl warm broth and tea with honey and arranged garlic cloves to nurse her daughter through a bad cold. From the overstuffed chair, she scanned the dark, finally focusing her attention on the small lump her daughter made under the *pododeyalnik* on the bed beside her. A shallow rasping sounded from below the linen coverlet.

She leaned forward from where she'd been keeping vigil and peeled back the blanket to caress Nadezhda's forehead. When she stroked her daughter's near-white curls from around her thin face, she yanked back her hand. The child's skin had seared her fingers

The girl cracked her eyes and winced. "Hot, Mommy. I'm hot."

Her lids fluttered shut, and she drifted back into a too-deep sleep.

Alexandra bit her lip to stifle the cry. Her worst fear had been realized. *Pneumonia.* She knew the signs only too well after her mother's own battle with the disease just a year ago.

As quickly and quietly as possible, she sped across the parquet hallway to her bedroom. In the doorway, she stopped and listened to Yuri's steady breaths and compared them to their daughter's ragged ones. She chewed her lip again as she debated whether to wake him. His recent unemployment had made his moods so unpredictable. She never knew whether he would lash out or cry in despair when he received bad news. A glance back to the other room determined her choice.

At his side, she again paused before placing a hand on his shoulder. His thin frame, so like Nadezhda's, rose and dropped rhythmically beneath it. She jiggled his shoulder.

He shuddered and squinted at her. "Alexandra?"

"It's Nadezhda," she said, her voice low, but urgent. "She needs to go to the hospital. Now."

He frowned. "Are you sure it can't wait until morning?"

She twisted her hands behind her back, reading his thoughts in the lines on his forehead. Since Viru-Preparat dismissed him from his research position six months ago, they'd lived on their savings and the meager benefits the government gave them for Nadezhda's disability. Between her mother's and their daughter's illnesses, they knew all too well how the medical system worked under the new market economy — emergency room, doctors, medicine. Fees. Fees. Fees. Yuri had to be adding it all up in his head.

She checked over her shoulder to the other bedroom, recalling the rattle with each of her daughter's breaths, and shook her head. "Her lips are blue. I lost my mother last winter because we waited. We can't risk it."

His gaze fixed on hers. She clenched her fingers tighter, waiting his response. The area around his eyes softened.

"Go. Meet me at the door."

With a tight nod, she sprinted from the room, shaking her hands to return the blood to them. In one movement, she scooped the child from the bed, blankets and all, and joined Yuri at their front door. As soon as he'd shrugged on his coat, he held out his arms for the bundle, and she put on her own wrap.

Their boots echoed through the building's narrow stairwell, then thudded on the courtyard's frozen mud as they crossed to the corrugated metal container holding their prize possession — a dull green Lada automobile.

Yuri grunted as he shoved back the top to reveal the car. Once they'd settled inside, he played with the choke and the gas pedal for several minutes before the car's engine finally whined to life. With a lurch, he steered the car out of the small garage and over the icy ruts into the Siberian night.

Only a few other cars' headlights, resembling insects' yellow eyes, flashed past them along the way. When their auto slid to a stop at the hospital's only entrance, a guard shuffled out of his shack and around the bar blocking their way.

Yuri opened the window, frigid air slicing through the crack. "This is urgent. Our daughter has pneumonia."

The guard's breath formed puffs of white in the car's headlights. "They're closed for an emergency disinfection. Go to the regional hospital."

"But that's a hundred kilometers from here."

The guard shrugged. "No one's here. All the doctors are on holiday."

The muscles in Yuri's face tightened, and she imagined him ticking off the additional costs: gasoline, wear on the tires, antifreeze, oil replacement, and on and on. How had they come to this point?

Before she could open her mouth to argue the need to make the trip, he shifted into reverse and headed back to the main road out of town. After the car turned onto the highway toward the regional capital, her attention swung between Nadezhda's breathing and the car's erratic course. Birch tree trunks flashed in the headlights as they sped past.

Yuri gripped the steering wheel, his knuckles white in the dashboard's glow. He caught her eye. "There's a lot of ice."

The child fidgeted in her arms, and she murmured quiet assurances to her before she did the same to her husband. "We'll get there."

As if to dispute her mother's assertions, Nadezhda fell into a coughing fit. Loud, wet hacks doubled her small frame. At first, Alexandra feared they would never quit. When they did, she held her breath until the child took a long, ragged inhale of her own.

The car's engine revved higher as they passed a sign noting the turnoff to the regional capital.

When they reached the hospital, Yuri yanked the wheel, and the car's tires jumped the curb in front of the main entrance's cracked steps. Without a word, he jerked open the car door and carried their daughter inside, leaving Alexandra to follow. Just inside the second set of doors, a guard slept behind a desk. A small TV set cast a blue light over his face, and smoke curled from a cigarette smoldering in an ashtray. Yuri pulled to a halt at the desk and cleared his throat. The guard snored on. After a short wait, he handed the child to Alexandra and tapped the man on his shoulder.

The guard peered at the three of them through one cracked eyelid. "*Da?*"

"This is an emergency. My daughter can't breathe."

With a sigh, the man opened both eyes, pulled out a smudged telephone list, shook a cigarette from a package on the desk, stuck it in his mouth, lit it with the butt from the ashtray, and picked up the telephone receiver. He spun the rotary dial three times, muttered into the mouthpiece, and hung up.

"The emergency entrance is on the other side, but I've called them for you. Wait. They'll come here." A puff of blue smoke flowed out with his words. He settled back into his chair and shut his eyes again.

Alexandra searched the waiting area for some place to sit. Spotting a wooden bench below a board listing doctors' names and work hours, she slumped onto it. With the bundle of blanket and child on her lap, she rocked back and forth in time to her husband's pacing on the curling linoleum.

The guard had long since fallen back to sleep by the time a large woman in a rumpled uniform entered from a back hallway. Her peroxided hair stuck out at odd angles from a lopsided nurse's cap. Approaching Alexandra, she held out her arms. "Give me the child. You can fill out the forms at the emergency entrance."

Alexandra watched Yuri turn to leave, but she remained seated, her daughter clutched to her chest. "No. I'm going with her. My husband will fill out the forms for you if you wish."

She ignored Yuri's stare when he spun back around.

The nurse jammed her hands onto her hips and shook her head. "No one's allowed in. Go. Fill out the papers. Then go home. Call after nine o'clock, and we'll let you know her status."

She reached for the child, and Alexandra leaned backward, lifting her chin to the nurse. This woman would not intimidate her. "She has a heart condition. I must speak with the doctor. Lead the way. I'll follow."

"I told you, it's not allowed. I won't be fined for breaking the sanitation rules."

Alexandra knew this objection all too well. Ministry of Health regulations barred all outsiders, including family, from visiting patients — as if hospitals could arrest and control illness like a criminal. Fathers' first glimpses of their newborn children were from maternity-ward courtyards. New mothers would hold a bundle to a window while the men peered upward and waved flowers at their wives.

But Alexandra also knew her daughter's care depended as much on her personal efforts to secure what the child needed as any doctor's skill. Avoiding Yuri's gaze, she fished some bills from her coat pocket and flashed them at the woman. "This should cover any fines."

The woman checked the bills she held out, snatched them from her, and stuffed them down the front of her uniform. "All right. You can come, but take off your boots." She spun on her heel and marched to the hallway entrance.

From her station by the door, the woman tapped her plastic sandal and glared at Alexandra as she stepped over to her husband and kicked off her boots.

"Take these with you," she told him. "I'll see you at the emergency entrance after we're settled."

"Alex — "

She placed a finger on his lips. "Not now." She shot a quick glance at the nurse. "Please. We'll talk about the money later."

His gaze met hers, and she knew a protest lay on his tongue, but he simply peeled back the blanket and kissed the top of their daughter's head. "I'll see you at the other entrance."

She shifted the blanket onto her shoulder and followed the nurse through the door. Inside the hospital proper, her stockinged feet slipped on the floor as she struggled to keep pace with the nurse through the twisting corridors. The hallway's faded beige walls had soaked up years of disinfectant, and its smell burned her nose and the back of her throat.

Faded paintings of Pushkin's fairy tale characters marked the walls of the children's ward. Just past a rendition of Baba Yaga's bird-foot house, the nurse turned into a room. In the semidarkness, Alexandra spied several metal-framed beds arranged like those in a military barracks, each holding a rolled-up mattress. At the first one, the nurse untied the mattress and made the bed with the set of sheets and blankets bundled inside.

Laying her daughter in the bed, Alexandra pulled the covers up to her chin.

"Will she be receiving oxygen?"

"The doctor has to order that. She'll be here shortly to examine her. Go join your husband. Come back after nine o'clock. The doctor will see you then."

She pulled off her coat and sat down next to her daughter. "I'm staying."

The nurse shrugged and left.

Now alone, she let her gaze rested on the child's face. Despite the fever, Nadezhda had a bluish tinge that gave her a peaceful, ethereal look. She wrapped a blond tendril around her finger and blinked back the tears stinging her eyelids.

A woman in a white coat and tall, white hat tiptoed to the other side of the bed and whispered, "I'm Dr. Volkova, the pediatrician on duty tonight. You say your daughter has pneumonia?"

Alexandra stood to address the doctor. "Her breathing became labored, so we drove her here. She has a congenital heart condition too."

She watched the doctor uncover the girl and open her nightshirt to listen to her chest. Her throat tightened when she saw the doctor's forehead crease.

"Her lungs are very congested. We'll begin the few antibiotics we have in stock right away. I'll have the nurse arrange a special room with oxygen for her."

"What about her heart?"

The doctor turned to stare out the window into the black night beyond. "I'm not a specialist. One can look at her in the morning. Right now, I want to focus on her breathing. I'll give you a list of antibiotics to buy. Bring them with you in the morning."

"Buy? Won't the government supply them?"

"Our budget has no funds for imported medicines." The doctor's lips pulled tight. "I've worked for two months now with no pay. Last week, they offered bathrobes instead of cash. What am I to do with twenty bathrobes? I'm a physician, not a street merchant. The staff turned down the offer and received nothing instead. Patients are on their own as much as we are. Be prepared to pay even more if her condition worsens."

Alexandra swallowed, Yuri's rants echoing in her head. She

couldn't take another row with him. Not tonight. "Of course. I'll take the list to my husband. He's waiting in the emergency room. I'm staying with her."

Dr. Volkova opened her mouth, but Alexandra preempted another argument about the sanitation rules, deciding to play her final card. "At hospital one twenty-two, they always allowed me to stay with her. My background in microbiology proved useful."

Her connection to the Soviet biological weapons factory in the former secret city registered in the doctor's face. She shut her mouth.

Alexandra continued. "I'm sure you can arrange for me to stay. There must be an extra bed somewhere."

"*Da.*" Volkova drew out the vowel. "I can see about a bed in your daughter's room, but don't interfere with the staff."

Before Alexandra could ask again about the specialist, Nadezhda gasped. With a jerk, her back arched and lifted her off the bed. The doctor ran to the door and called for help.

By the time the doctor returned to Nadezhda's side, the nurse had arrived, pushing a cart filled with glass bottles in front of her. She and the doctor worked over the child, the nurse shoving shunts the size of knitting needles into her arms.

Alexandra felt the blood rush from her head and feared she might collapse.

"What is it? What's happening?"

Glancing in her direction, the doctor barked at the nurse "Get her out of here. Now."

The nurse sprinted toward her and dragged her from the room.

"Please. What's the matter with her?"

Her begging received only a shake from the nurse's head as she continued forcing her toward the door. "No time to talk now. Join your husband. The doctor will see you there."

Before she could protest again, the door closed in her face.

Even though the lock clicked into place, she grabbed the knob and twisted, shoving her body against the door. The doctor's shouts carried into the hallway, but she could make no sense of them. Fear and frustration, held at bay through the long ride, flooded over her. She clung to the doorknob and allowed the tears to flow.

Chapter Two

*H*is quarry was leaving. Sergei Borisov gave his cigarette one last puff and dropped it to the sidewalk. Focusing his gaze on the target's back, he ignored the others who passed between them on the street. Gray-coated *babushkas* ambled along, string bags loaded with the day's purchases hanging from their arms. Grizzle-bearded men trailed foul-smelling cigarette smoke. Young Russians in fur coats chattered away on cellular phones. He continued his pursuit at a safe distance and shifted his gaze briefly to the sky. The Siberian sun made only a white circle in the heavy gray hanging over the rooftops. The wind changed, picked up speed, and stung his cheeks pink.

He always enjoyed this part of the chase — this game of wolf and rabbit — because he excelled at it. His round face, short fair hair, and lean body made him nondescript enough to become the department's best shadow. More importantly, he had the patience, a skill mastered early in life. Pity that the precision setting him above the others in his office also held him back. Attention to detail required time — time not spent nurturing relationships within the bureaucracy. Politics and glad-handing weren't his style. Why couldn't those fools at the top see his way led to true results? Unfortunately, promotions seemed to go to the backslappers rather than those making arrests.

His subject stopped and checked behind him. Sergei turned, pretending to study a window display of imported perfumes, something not even heard of in this country only a few years ago. Behind his reflection, he saw the man glance about as if to orient himself, turn, and head down a walkway under the street. Once out on the other side, he scurried back along the street in the direction he'd come.

Sergei kept his target in sight and continued his earlier catalog of the changes in Stop-100 since the KGB became the FSB. Infrastructure had been bad enough under Communist rule, but ten years of economic reform had left it to rot from within. Like other formerly closed cities, it now offered little to residents. The wide sidewalks and even wider avenues suffered from potholes and crumbling cement that made both driving and walking difficult. Since Gogol's times, Russia had been famous for bad roads. Democracy hadn't changed that.

Snowflakes began to fall. Big, fat feathers dropped on everything on the street, decorating all with a white frosting. He hated winter in this backwater town. In weaker moments, he'd admit to himself he'd been tempted to leave the bureau, but the alternative appealed to him even less. He'd watched the flashy ones leave to form private security firms and protect the same ones they would've investigated the week before. In those dark moments, he reminded himself that guarding some New Russian who'd made his money in very shady ways and might or might not deserve to continue living did not compare with serving the nation as a whole.

Sergei rounded a corner and spotted the man farther up the street. For the next half hour, his rabbit backtracked and crossed streets. Sergei let the distance between them increase. He knew now the man headed toward the warehouse district. Tall, grimy concrete buildings gave way to shorter, wooden ones. Behind awkwardly leaning fences, the structures' dull, metal roofs blended with the gray sky.

After the man turned one corner, Sergei pulled a radio out of his pocket and reported his location to Yevgeny, his commander. When he, too, turned the corner, he stopped for just a second. The man had vanished, but a single set of footprints in the snow marked his trail along a deserted side street. Sergei couldn't resist the smirk. Some criminal mastermind. Even Yevgeny, the latest idiot to be promoted over him, would've been able to track this one.

Sergei approached the entrance at an angle and checked the

lock. The latch responded to his tug, but he feared the rusted hinges might warn those inside if he opened the door too far. He cracked it and heard snatches of some foreign language drift out with the musty air. Slowly, he stepped back from the door. Once a safe distance away, he radioed the order, hoping Yevgeny would be smart enough to keep the sirens silent.

Within minutes, a canvas-covered truck careened onto the street and screeched to a halt in front of him. The dull green cover flew up to reveal seven helmeted men in fatigues. Part of the elite OMON team, their military training and appearance made them both terrifying and efficient. They turned expectantly toward Sergei. He nodded and pointed to the still-opened door.

The first trooper trotted to the entrance and jerked the door back so sharply its hinges snapped with a crack. The others ran through, rifles ready. Excited shouts and quick, heavy boot falls echoed in the building's cavernous emptiness.

Sergei followed just behind them. By the time he'd caught up with them, two men lay on the ground. Both wore almost identical heavy wool coats and dark fur hats — far more clothing than someone used to the weather would wear. With their faces pointed to the ground, Sergei couldn't see their features, but knew they weren't Russian.

The one he'd tracked lay perfectly still, several rifles pointed at his head, a trooper's heavy boot crushing it into the gritty floor. The other man lay spread-eagle next to the first and babbled in broken Russian about diplomatic immunity. He tried to raise himself. Another boot came down with a thud on his back. He hit the floor with a gasp.

"What's he saying?" a voice behind Sergei asked.

He snapped to attention as Yevgeny stepped next to him. The scent of his imported cigarette overpowered the warehouse's musty odor.

Why did he always feel like the country serf next to this man? He took in his commander's Italian wool coat, leather shoes, and sable hat. His own Russian-made clothing appeared coarse and ill-fitting next to his superior's. Yevgeny had to be on someone's payroll, but he was hardly alone. Besides himself, Sergei couldn't think of anyone who wasn't above taking a little on the side to help make ends meet.

"Something about diplomatic immunity."

He left off the "sir." Until a few weeks ago, they'd been the same rank.

His new boss frowned and took another puff on the cigarette. "Is that possible?"

Without meeting Yevgeny's gaze, he said, "I guess so. He could be working for an embassy. Whether he can be prosecuted would be up to others."

Yevgeny's brow furrowed deeper. He stared over Sergei's shoulder into the warehouse's shadows. "Is that the equipment over there?"

Without waiting for a reply, his supervisor strolled to where he had focused. His leather-soled shoes made a soft, gritting sound that echoed and amplified throughout the space. Sergei followed him. Passing the troopers, Yevgeny nodded to them, and they pulled the two men to their feet and handcuffed them. He stopped in front of the large, steel cylinders just as Sergei caught up with him. Tubing protruded from the top and different places on the sides. Their ends had been crudely sawed. Crusty streaks and corrosion coated the seams.

"You've been investigating this theft from where?" Yevgeny asked.

"One of the institutes. The budget cuts made them dismiss personnel. Fewer personnel means less equipment needed. And the Iranians are paying premium prices for such things. It appears the institute's director made quite a lucrative deal on this one."

He decided not to share that the seller had already left the country, having completed this one last deal before absconding with his profits.

"Well, we've just made a dent in the Iranians' efforts to get them," Yevgeny said with a self-satisfied smile.

"Perhaps."

He faced him. "You're not convinced?"

Sergei considered his options before replying. Just how much should he share? He never fully trusted or respected the man — even if he was now his superior. "This is just part of the troika. Besides equipment, they need personnel and…seed."

Yevgeny's confused expression didn't raise Sergei's opinion. Had this man read a single one of his reports?

With a sigh, Sergei explained. "The starter virus. That's what this equipment's for. To grow more virus from the seed. We've stopped the export of some equipment like these pieces. The personnel, we're watching. That leaves the seed. Without the starter virus, they wouldn't be able to make anything."

"Maybe that's where we need to concentrate. On the seed."

How astute.

Sergei sucked in his breath to keep from grimacing when the man pounded him companionably on his shoulder.

"Keep up the good work. You'll get promoted yet. I'll leave you to clean up here. See you back at the office."

Sergei watched the man leave and rubbed his arm. He knew how Yevgeny the politician would spin the tale of this arrest, and it drained all satisfaction of a job well done right out of him.

Chapter Three

Alexandra lay on the hard ground. Rocks dug into her back. She shifted, but they still poked and prodded her, grinding through her skin. She opened her eyes and stared into the yellow ones of a she-wolf. Somehow, Alexandra knew it was female. She tried to scream, but the sound froze in her throat. The wolf, in response, narrowed her eyes and opened her mouth, revealing two rows of long, white fangs. To Alexandra's surprise, no growl followed, only a hiss like a snake.

Her eyes popped open. With the image of the dream wolf still in her thoughts, she scanned the area around her for signs of danger. She shifted and heard the squeak of rusted metal. Bedsprings. The rocks were bedsprings poking her through a thin mattress. She sat up, now fully alert as she remembered the night ride to the hospital.

After throwing back her bedcovers, she tiptoed to Nadezhda's side. The wolf's hiss grew louder. Oxygen flowed through a tube encircling her daughter's face just under her nose. She pushed back the girl's hair, letting her hand rest on her forehead. The antibiotic drip was working. Her skin felt cooler.

Nadezhda squirmed, whimpering deep in her throat, and Alexandra removed her hand. How long had she slept? Had anyone checked on her daughter since they'd moved her to the current room? Helplessness overwhelmed her. She knew so much about what caused disease. She could see the image of the pneumococcal bacteria in her mind and describe the disease's progression, and knew the procedures to create the vaccines and antibiotics to prevent them. Unfortunately, she had to rely on others for treatment.

She stole to the door, the floor cold against her bare feet, and eased it open to peek outside. From far down the deserted hallway, she could hear the clinking of plates and metal silverware and the distinct smell of boiled kasha. Her stomach growled. When had she last eaten? She remembered Yuri trying to coax her to eat some soup yesterday afternoon. Her stomach grumbled again. Would they even think to offer her any food? She knew they would be willing to *sell* her some.

After closing the door as softly as she could, she leaned against it. Her argument with Yuri over staying at the hospital returned, and she covered her ears to block his harangue about how much it cost. The door moved behind her. Someone on the other side pushed hard, shoving the knob into a particularly sore spot in her back. With a sharp squeal of pain, she jumped away from the door.

A head poked through the crack in the door. "Sorry."

Her startled expression gave way to a smile. "Vladimir, it's so good to see you."

She stepped aside to let one of her oldest and dearest friends pass. Vladimir, Yuri, and she had been inseparable since their youth.

"Did I hurt you?"

"No, just took me by surprise."

He drew her to him with a strong hug, and she peered behind him. "Did Yuri come with you?"

He shuffled his feet. "He wanted to, but he told me they'd put him on some sort of list. I understand the security guard escorted him out after your argument with him about the medicines. I offered to bring them to you."

"He's so temperamental lately," she said with a shake of her head. "Always getting into trouble. But how did you convince them to let you in?"

He gave her a wicked grin, a sign he'd been up to his old mischief again. "It turns out the head nurse is single…"

"That old witch? You charmed her?" Her voice rose in shock.

Used to his good looks, she'd always been amazed at how easily others fell under his spell. Few women could resist his athletic body and expressive blue eyes. Even as a teenager, he'd been able to talk his way out of trouble more than once.

"Here's what the doctor requested," he said and handed her a small plastic bag. "And your mother-in-law gave me these."

He held up a brown paper bag stained with grease spots.

Without opening the bag, she could smell her mother-in-law's homemade cabbage pies. "*Pirozhkii*," she said with a smile. She reached inside the bag. "And they're still warm. How nice of her to think of me. She's so thoughtful."

She fished one pie out of the bag and finished it in three bites. Vladimir's question made her stop licking her fingers. "And what has the doctor said this morning?"

"I haven't seen her yet today."

He frowned. "That's unacceptable. She must check on her." He turned toward the door.

"Where are you going?"

He faced her, that telltale smirk on his lips. "To find the doctor, of course."

"Please, don't make a fuss." She placed her hand on his arm. "She let me stay, and I don't want her — "

He raised a hand. "My dear, don't worry. I'll be respectful."

With a quick spin, he pulled away from her grasp and strode from the room. She let the door shut quietly behind him. Stopping him would be futile. Once he made up his mind, no one could change it. She knew of only one time in his life he'd not gotten his way.

Nadezhda stirred behind her, and she rushed to her side. "Mommy?" she asked as her eyes fluttered open.

"Yes, dear. I'm right here. You're very sick and in the hospital."

"No. Don't like hospitals. Want to go home."

"I know, dear, but you can't go home right now. As soon as you are better — "

"Don't want to stay."

Her face reddened, and Alexandra feared the exertion could worsen her condition. "Please, my little Hope, don't cry. How about I tell you a story?" The girl gave a nod, and she began the tale. "A long time ago in a faraway land…"

Before the princess and prince even met, Nadezhda's eyelids drooped, and she dozed again. Alexandra pulled the blanket up to her daughter's chin once again, careful to avoid disturbing the needles stuck in her arms. The child's continued sleep concerned her. What was in the fluid dripping into her daughter's arm? She checked the IV bottle. It was almost empty.

The door opened behind her, and Vladimir gave her a big grin when she turned. "The doctor will be here momentarily. She's arranging for the specialist to see Nadezhda."

"What did you say to her?"

"Just the truth," he said with a shrug. "That she's the granddaughter of a national hero and should be treated as such."

Her mouth dropped open. "Vladimir, you didn't. We're not supposed to — "

"All I said was your father received a medal."

"The laboratory explosion is a matter of national security. Even my mother never told me — "

He placed a hand on her shoulder. "Please, let me take care of this. You concern yourself with Nadezhda. Her heart may be weak, but her will is strong. That's why you named her Hope."

She dropped her gaze. "It's times like these I regret leaving Viru-Preparat. At least we had access to other specialty hospitals besides the one in Stop-100."

"You made the right decision. Who knows what you were exposed to there? The peroxide in the air turned everyone's hair the same color as yours." He took a lock resting on her shoulder between his fingers and studied it carefully.

"Things are so bad." She shook her head, and the strand slipped from his grasp. "I saw Piotr the other day. He's lost his job too. They seem to be letting everyone go. I wonder who will be left. You were smart to leave so early. Look at how well you've done." She sighed. "I wish we had your business sense."

"Few do." His smile was faint, but the pride obvious. "But you seem to be learning. You've got that wolf of a doctor under control."

His play on Dr. Volkova's name brought a faint smile to her lips as well. It drooped just as quickly when the pediatrician appeared in the doorway as if summoned.

"The specialist will examine her in an hour," she said without stepping in the room and retreating hastily.

"I do believe she's afraid of us," he said, his smirk clearly visible this time.

Before Alexandra could give him a good-natured reprimand, Nadezhda stirred again. As before, she sprinted to her side and smoothed her hand across the child's brow, whispering to her to stay still.

The girl tossed her head from side to side. "Want to go home, Mommy. Please."

"You will, my dear. You will. As soon as you're better."

"And you'll stay with me?"

She exchanged a frown with Vladimir over her daughter's head. His slight nod told her he would convince Yuri she needed to remain in the hospital. Turning back to Nadezhda, she said, "Of course. If you'll stay still, I'll finish my story."

"The one about the princess?"

"If you wish."

"Start at the beginning."

"All right. Along time ago in a faraway land — "

She paused and raised her gaze, but Vladimir had disappeared.

"Mommy, my story."

"Sorry. A princess named…?"

"Nadezhda."

"On a particular day, a princess named Nadezhda was very, very happy…"

Spinning the custom-made tale, she felt herself relax. Vladimir's visit had assured her of his support as well as Yuri's, and she knew Nadezhda would need all three's efforts to bring her home.

❧

In the dim stairwell leading from the children's ward to the hospital's first floor, Alexandra tugged on her skirt to smooth out the wrinkles. She'd glimpsed at herself in the ward's mottled bathroom mirror. Dark circles under her eyes made her cheeks appear particularly pale. She'd tried to fix her hair by running herwet fingers through it, but only succeeded in making her curls droop in strings about her face.

At the bottom of the stairs, she stopped and forced a smile. Yuri waited on the other side of the door in front of her. Vladimir had managed to smooth things with the hospital administration enough to allow Yuri access to the doctors' consultation offices.

Good.

Nadezhda needed his support as much as hers. Taking a deep breath, Alexandra pushed through the door and found him clasping a small bag at his side. His smile faltered when he saw her. The bathroom mirror obviously didn't do justice to her disheveled appearance.

His smile returned when she approached him and kissed him softly. "It's good to see you. Nadezhda keeps asking about you."

He hugged her. "How is she?"

"Resting better now. I think they may let her go home in a day or two."

Yuri's face darkened. Did he know something he hadn't shared? "Let's find out what the heart specialist has to say. He's waiting for us in the director's office."

He linked his arm through hers as they stepped along the hallway.

"Thank you for sending the medicines with Vladimir." She squeezed his arm. "Are those more?"

He glanced at the string bag in his other hand. "No. It's a gift for the specialist. Vladimir helped me get it."

"He's been a good friend. His persistence got the specialist here to see her. I don't know how we'll repay him."

His arm stiffened under her grip, and she shot a glance at his face, as rigid as his arm. What had she said to put him off? Before she could ask more, he opened a door, and they stepped into the office.

Inside, a large woman with frizzled hair sat behind a desk stacked high with files and folders. She munched on a pickle as she shuffled the papers from one pile to another. Behind her, a large window provided a view of snow-frosted trees in the hospital's courtyard. When had it snowed?

"We're here to see Dr. Filipov," Yuri said when the woman raised her head and peeked over the stacks on her desk.

"The next room," she said, pointing at a door with the pickle. "He's waiting for you."

Yuri let Alexandra pass through first, and the contrast from the secretary's sunlit office to the dark paneled one disoriented her. Her eyes finally focused on a small man with a round, balding head and a pair of black reading glasses perched near the end of his nose. A file folder lay open in front of him, Nadezhda's name written sideways in large, black letters on the file tab. He kept his head down as if studying it.

She continued across the red rug in front of the desk to one of two straight-backed chairs. Yuri took the seat next to her. When they received no acknowledgment, she asked, "You are Dr. Filipov?"

The man lifted his gaze from the desk and studied them over his glasses. "Yes."

"Dr. Filipov." Yuri shifted and cleared his throat. "I would like to thank you for examining our daughter and offer you this gift in appreciation of your kind attention."

He pulled a bottle of vodka from the string bag. Filipov accepted it and studied the label. Even from her seat, she could tell it was imported. Vladimir's taste showed through again. Alexandra twisted her hands in her lap. Their child's life depended on this man, and it all boiled down to a bottle of vodka?

"Thank you very much. I'll enjoy this later," he said and put the bottle on the floor beside him. "I've been reviewing your daughter's file. I won't lie to you. The conclusions at this point are not optimistic."

She untwisted her hands and reached across the space between the chairs to grab Yuri's.

The doctor took off his glasses. Placing his hands, fingers spread wide, over the papers on the desk, he said, "This bout of pneumonia has weakened her heart. How severely, we can't know without further tests. She'll need to go to a specialty hospital."

"And what will you be able to do for her? After the tests?" Yuri asked in a harsh whisper.

The doctor frowned. "Depending on the severity of the strain on her heart, it might be correctable with medication or an operation."

"Specialty hospitals. Operations." Yuri let go of her hand and ran his fingers through his hair. "Such things are expensive now."

Money again. She searched for a way to make it more palatable to Yuri. "Surely the government will provide some help with these costs?"

"Possibly," Filipov said. He leaned back in his chair. "Petition the Ministry of Health. They sometimes agree to provide care. I would suggest you request the Cardiology Institute in Moscow. The best surgeons are there."

"You mean where President Yeltsin was treated?" she asked.

A list of the people she knew to help her with the petition formed in her mind. As always Vladimir's father appeared toward the top of the list. A representative to Russia's Parliament, Vladimir's father had the Moscow connections to make the admission happen.

"I would also suggest you consider another option." The doctor cleared his throat. "Consider placing the girl in a sanatorium. Caring for such a child at home must be a burden — both physical and financial. Surely you desire more children. It would not be fair for them if you focus all your attention on one sick child."

The heat of an old anger rushed through her. Since their daughter's birth, she'd heard this argument and refused to listen to the same rubbish from one more "expert," no matter how well-intentioned. Her chair clattered to the floor behind her when she leaped to her feet.

"No." Her hands fisted at her sides, and she chose her words carefully. "That is *not* an option. We've seen those…places. I won't let her go there as long as I have any say in the matter. She is not something to be replaced…like an old shoe. She is our daughter."

Filipov stood, his face darkening. Mother and doctor glared at each other until she broke away to glance at Yuri for his support.

He rose. "Please, Dr. Filipov, excuse my wife. Nadezhda's illness has been difficult for both of us. You know, of course, we're most grateful for your advice. We will certainly revisit the idea. In the meantime, we would appreciate your help in arranging for her transfer to a specialty hospital."

His words stunned her to the quick. Had he just apologized for her reaction? How could he side with this idiot? Yuri reached behind her and straightened the chair. She offered no resistance when he took her arm and forced her back into her seat.

"Of course." Dr. Filipov's expression softened at Yuri's actions. "You've both been under a great deal of stress. These times challenge us all. I'm sure we'll be able to work out something. Our budgets are tight, but we don't turn away a sick child because of money. Besides, we're discussing the worst situation. Maybe she'll not need an operation."

He readjusted the glasses on his nose and closed the file, signaling the end of their discussion. Alexandra popped up from her chair, a thousand questions on the tip of her tongue, but Yuri's stare silenced them all. Once again, immobilized by his response, she followed his lead and offered her hand to the doctor.

Outside in the corridor, Yuri turned on her. "You almost ruined everything. Do you realize how hard I worked to get a gift for that man for examining her? Not to mention the medicines? What favors Vladimir and I pulled?"

She glanced up the hallway. Two nurses chatted cheerily with each other as they advanced toward them. At Yuri's outburst, they stopped several feet away, eyeing them suspiciously, as if afraid to pass.

"I'm sorry," she said in a low voice. "I should've realized what you've been going through."

He paced the floor. "And now there'll be even more medicines to buy," he said aloud, more to himself than to her. "Not to mention tests. Specialists."

He turned to her, taking her shoulders in his hands. "How're we going to pay for it?"

Dropping her gaze, she studied her stockinged feet. A toe stuck out of a hole in one wool sock. Lifting her head, she said in a small but determined voice, "I don't know. But we have to. I can't lose her."

"She's my daughter too." His sigh told her how heavy he felt their burden to be. "I know what we decided when she was born — about the sanatorium. But things have changed." He took her hands. "We could put her in one. Just temporarily. The government would care for her, and we needn't worry how to pay for it or the medicines."

She closed her eyes. At the urging of more than one specialist, they'd visited several homes for sick children. Regardless of the institution's reputation or affiliation, they found the staff kept the facility neat to the point of sterility. At one, the director had proudly showed them the latest didactic materials, pristine and carefully locked in glass cases, safe from children's curious fingers. After seeing how the facilities served as warehouses rather than providing true care, they decided they could do better at home, and Alexandra had quit her job.

Her eyes wide, she pulled back from him. "How can you even

suggest — ”

"Because I can see the truth." His face clouded. "Things don't change just by hoping."

"Do you truly believe the staff at some sanatorium will ensure she gets the care she needs? Would one of them sit by her bed and watch over her?"

"You know I want the best for her, just like you, but we made that decision four years ago. We have fewer resources than we did then — ”

She shook her head violently as if to block the words from entering her ears. "*Nyet. Nyet.* We decided. We're not going to talk about this again."

"You will listen to me." His lips formed a thin line. "From the beginning we've accepted her illness as our responsibility. We may never know whether her bad heart developed because of us, of what we exposed ourselves to in the labs. But we must be realistic. We no longer have the same *svyazi*, the same influence — or money — we used to have. We'll wait to see what the other tests say, but we must be prepared to make another decision."

She shuddered, his words ice water in her face. "I won't abandon her. Don't force me to choose. My decision may not please you."

Running from him, she pushed past the two nurses and through the stairway door. He would never follow her. For him, rules were rules. But for her, when Nadezhda was involved, rules were merely obstacles to be overcome with money or influence or whatever other means necessary. Regardless the results of this latest problem, she would once again find a way to solve it — just as she'd done in the past.

Chapter Four

*T*he next few weeks for Sergei turned out to be even worse than he'd imagined. By the time he finally got back to his office at the local FSB building, Yevgeny had already bragged to one and all about the great arrest he, Yevgeny, had supervised. Sergei, if mentioned, appeared only as a footnote in the whole affair.

After days of praise for Yevgeny's magnificent arrest, the gossip shifted, and Sergei's name appeared more prominently in the recounting. Not one, but both of the arrested men were connected with the Iranian embassy, and Sergei's failure to check that detail ended their arrest. But he knew the true reason for his shift to office pariah. Despite Moscow's concerns over certain biological agents leaving the country, other interests, such as the sale of nuclear technology, forced the Kremlin to find it best for all concerned if the two foreigners left the country without prosecution. Within a week, the men were gone, and all Sergei had to show for his months of work was a hulk of equipment taking up space in the office basement.

After Yevgeny shared with him Moscow's instructions for returning the confiscated apparatus to the original institute, Sergei contemplated once more the idea of chucking his career — what was left of it after this latest fiasco — and joining a security firm someplace far from Moscow and Stop-100. Someplace warm, like

Sochi.

This idea gained even more appeal when he returned to his cubby of an office and found the unthinkable sitting behind his desk. An outsider — no, a *foreigner* — reclined in *his* chair behind *his* desk, idly browsing through the papers scattered on top. It was enough to make a loyal servant of the Motherland reach for the job listings.

The warped floorboards creaked, announcing his arrival. "Can I help you with something, Marcus?"

His uninvited guest glanced up and beamed at him. Sergei could never get the image of the Marlboro Man out of his mind whenever Marcus Gordon appeared. Although Marcus wore snow boots and no hat, Sergei could easily see him dressed like the cowboy in the ads, riding a horse and whooping at a bunch of cows. The CIA agent's loud, friendly attitude always set Sergei's teeth on edge. The old swivel chair groaned as Marcus shoved it back to stand. "I heard about the bust," he said in gruff, heavily accented Russian. He heaved his thick frame between the wall and desk and held out his hand. "Congratulations."

Sergei grasped the outstretched hand, and Marcus pumped it like he was extracting oil. "Bust?" Sergei recalled no explosion occurring in the area.

"Collar?" Marcus asked.

Sergei continued to stare, unable to determine what the man was talking about.

Exasperation tinged Marcus's next question. "Well, what do you call an arrest?"

Sergei pushed past him to the other side of the desk and tossed some report forms on its top. "An arrest."

"Then congratulations on the arrest."

"Thanks," Sergei said without enthusiasm. "You may be the only one who still considers it a victory. The whole thing fell to pieces once the politicians got involved."

"Heard about them letting those *diplomats* go." Marcus sat in the straight-back chair on the other side of the desk. It protested even louder than the swivel chair but held his weight. "Predictable."

Sergei waited for him to put his feet up on the desk, but the man merely leaned back and stretched his legs in front of him.

"All bureaucracies are the same," Marcus said. "When the

ones at the top interfere, the whole thing goes to shit. I can't help you with that case, but maybe I can help you out with another arrest. Take a look at this fellow."

He pulled a photo out of his suit coat pocket and handed it to him.

Sergei sat down and studied the grainy black-and-white picture. A swarthy man with a few days' growth of beard and black, curly hair passed through airport customs. He could have been Chechen or from any of the southern republics.

Sergei dropped the photo to his desk. "Who is he?"

"First name's Ahmed. His last name we're not sure about. Came in on a Turkish passport, but the last name on that one is not the same as the one on another passport. An *Iranian* passport. And he's no diplomat."

"What's he doing here?"

"So far, nothing. At least not that we can figure out. I'm here because we've trailed him to this region. You should be watching him too."

"Oh, I should?"

"Don't get sensitive. This is your jurisdiction so we're sharing some information with you."

"Sharing information?" Sergei stood and slapped his hands down on his desk. "You give me a picture of a man whose name you're not sure of, who's doing nothing so far, and tell me to watch him. You just want me to do your dirty work and then take the credit. You're no better than Yevgeny."

Marcus pulled himself from the chair and placed his beefy hands on the desk, just opposite Sergei's. He leaned so far forward Sergei could smell the onions the man had on his eggs for breakfast.

"Don't get your underpants in a bunch just because you feel you're not moving up in your department. We're on the same side here. Trying to stop certain things from going where we'd both prefer they never got. If you're not interested in this information, others in your agency are, and I'll give it to them."

The two faced off over the desk a moment. Slowly, Sergei's lips twitched upward. The CIA agent's fractured Russian was more than he could take. An image of his nylon briefs knotting between his legs formed in his mind. His smile broadened. He started laughing.

"Underpants in a bunch." He sputtered out the words between guffaws, tears forming in his eyes.

He sat back in his chair and swiped his eyes, his mirth dying to a chuckle. He raked his fingers through his short hair. "You're right. I'm sorry. The politics of this job get to me sometimes."

"It does to us all." Marcus smiled back at him. "I'm not even supposed to share what I have with you, but I know I can trust you to use it wisely."

He held out his hand. "Let me see the photo again."

Marcus passed it back to him. Setting his expression, Sergei began a mental review of the people he had seen during his surveillance of the men they had just arrested and released. He stopped at one image and compared it to the one in his hand. Possibly. Possibly.

With still no change in expression, he handed it back to Marcus. "I'll let you know if anything comes up."

"I'd appreciate that." The American stood and adjusted the belt around his waist. "I've got another appointment. Again, congratulations on your…arrest."

Sergei shook the man's hand over his desk. "I appreciate your trust."

"No problem. Remember, we're on the same side when it comes to this."

After the CIA agent's footsteps died away, Sergei picked up his phone's heavy receiver and called another internal extension.

"Pavel," he said, "I have a name to go with that man…Yes, that one…Ahmed…No, I don't have a last name, yet. But you'll find one soon enough."

Smiling to himself, he rang off. He wasn't going to let anyone, including the politicians, interfere with this case.

Chapter Five

$\mathcal{A}$lexandra stared at the few coins and crumpled ruble notes scattered on the bed. She'd expected more when she'd poured them from the pickle jar hidden under the bedroom floorboard. Like most Russians, she and Yuri didn't trust banks. In recent years, they had a tendency to collapse and leave depositors with nothing but a bankbook to an empty account. Only the rich, like Vladimir, used banks, and even then, only foreign ones where their money remained outside the country.

She smoothed the bills out and added them up along with the coins. Had they been robbed? Surely a thief would take it all and not leave such a pittance?

Footsteps pulled her out of her thoughts. She turned to her husband. "What happened to all our money?"

His jaw tightened. "You think all those medications are cheap? And the doctors and the hospital — "

"But we must have more than this? Before I left — "

"Are you questioning me? You think I stole it? Besides, even if I did use some of it, don't I have a right? I earned it from *my* job."

"But Nadezhda — "

"You have no idea what her bills are like. Who do you think has been paying them while you've been in the hospital with her?"

"I *had* to stay with her. To make sure the doctors saw her, and the nurses gave her her medications. And if Vladimir hadn't insisted on getting the heart specialist to see her — "

"Vladimir again." He pounded his fist into the palm of his other hand. "I'm so sick of hearing about his help. You'd think I was his assistant. *I* did all the visiting to the different pharmacies, searching for one medicine here, another one there because no one carried all of them. *I* bought the gifts for the doctors. All he did was to bring them to you."

"Because you couldn't be civil long enough to convince them to let you in. If you'd just — "

"If I hadn't calmed the specialist down that first day, you would've been kicked out as well."

"Enough." She waved her arms as if to clear the air of the angry words floating between them. "Our arguing is a cat's cry. I have to figure out how to pay for this trip to Moscow. All the papers are ready to petition the Ministry of Health. Vladimir has offered to help with the appointment. If I go there personally — "

"Planning to leave me alone again? What about Nadezhda? She just got out of the hospital."

"I'm not abandoning her or you. I'm just going to Moscow for a few days. I've already talked to Lena. We've kept in touch after she moved there. She's going to let me stay with her. But we obviously don't have enough for a plane ticket…or even a train ticket."

She looked about the room. "We'll just have to sell something."

"What have we got to sell?" He gave a little snort. "It's not like we haven't anything of value."

"There's the car…"

"You want to sell the only transportation we have?"

"No, I don't want to sell it. You asked what we have of value. I answered the question."

"We're not selling the car. I need it. *We* need it. How else would we have gotten to the hospital that night if we hadn't had a car?"

"I told you, I'm not interested in selling the car."

She did a quick mental inventory of their possessions. The apartment and their furnishings were modest, complemented by some small pieces her mother had brought with her when she'd moved in during her illness. They'd sold most of her belongings at that time to cover her medical expenses and later, the funeral expenses. Alexandra had so wanted to keep a few pieces of her mother's jewelry for Nadezhda, but neither her mother's nor hers had survived except for...she glanced down at her hands. The slender gold wedding band glinted at her. She raised her gaze to Yuri.

"I could sell my wedding band."

"You're not selling your ring."

"What difference does it make? We know we're married. Everyone knows we're married. It's not going to make a difference between us if I sell it — "

The area around his eyes folded, and his voice softened. "You don't understand. I worked extra hours to save for that ring. Every time I see it, I remember my sacrifice and love for you."

She touched the band, surprised how deeply this bit of news moved her as well. "Selling it won't change any of that. Don't you love Nadezhda too?"

He walked to her and placed his hands on her shoulders. When their gazes met, she saw tears glistening in his eyes. "Of course I do. Aren't we doing all this for her? But do you have to sell the one thing that symbolizes so much to me?"

"Then what about your ring?" She dropped her gaze. "It wouldn't bother me if you didn't wear it."

She reached up and pulled his hands off her shoulders. Still holding them in her own, she turned his palms upward and gasped. A band of white skin lined the third finger of his left hand. He curled his fingers under.

"You sold it? All this talk about love and symbols, and you'd already sold yours? I can't believe you."

He jerked his hands from hers and paced about the space between her and the bedroom door. "You just don't understand. I have expenses. We just can't wait for someone to give us money or a job. You have to go out and make it happen. That's what I've been doing. Making contacts, learning about business opportunities, investing in some of them."

"Is that what happened to our money?" Her voice rose. She glanced over her shoulder, remembering Nadezhda was playing in her bedroom across the hall. She forced her voice back to a normal tone. "What do we know of business? We're scientists. We know test tubes and incubators. Have you discussed these deals with

Vladimir? At least he — ”

He stared her down. "I could tell you a few things about Vladimir. He may charm you, but he doesn't fool me." He marched to her and grabbed her by the forearms. "I see how he looks at you when he doesn't know anyone's watching. The hunger in his eyes — ”

She twisted in his grasp, unable to meet his gaze. She knew what he meant, but had hoped he'd never seen it. "You don't know what you're talking about. He's just a friend. A good friend. When I think about all the help he's given us. How dare you accuse him of — ”

"He has you fooled," he said, gripping her harder. He studied her face. "Or maybe not. Maybe you do know, and that's why you're so willing to sell the ring."

"What are you saying? I love you, Yuri. I have since we were in high school."

"Do you?" His face softened, and his grip loosened. "Truly? Enough to forgive me for anything?"

"Of course." She pulled him close, pressing him to her. They'd been through so much. This was just the latest, but the question still nagged at her. She spoke softly, her face against the rough fabric of his shirt. "What have you done that you need my forgiveness?"

His body stiffened, and he pushed her back.

"I can't believe you. You never give up. Can't you let me have just one moment of peace without accusing me of something?"

"I was only asking because you said — ”

"I wasn't speaking of anything specific."

"Because if you mean your wedding ring — ”

"I told you it wasn't anything specific. We're just having a hard time right now and…just forget it."

He strode from the room. His footsteps continued toward the front door. She followed to catch him.

By the time she reached him, he'd already shoved his arms into his jacket. "You're going out again?"

He stomped his foot into one boot. "I'm not staying here and listen to your whining and accusations."

He stamped the other foot to secure its boot.

"Where are you going, Daddy?" Nadezhda stood in the middle of the hallway. Her left arm held a plastic doll in a chokehold. "Can I come too?"

The creases in his forehead deepened, and he shook his head. "Not this time."

Alexandra moved to where their daughter stood and knelt beside her. "You just got out the hospital, my dear. You shouldn't go out in the cold."

"Please stay, Daddy. Stay with me and Mommy. We can play tea party."

Alexandra shifted her gaze to his face, adding her own silent plea.

His jaw squared. "Later." With a yank, he opened the door and marched out, letting it close behind him with a bang.

"Is Daddy mad at me?" the little girl asked, tears glistening in her eyes.

"No, my dear," Alexandra said, blinking back her own tears. "He's just upset. He worried so much while you were in the hospital. Every time we spoke, the first thing he asked was 'How is our little Hope?'" She rose to her feet and took the girl's free hand in hers. "I'd love to play tea party."

"I have it all set up," she said, pulling her mother toward her bedroom. "You can be the daughter, and I'm the mother."

"All right, Mommy," Alexandra said, imitating a little girl's voice.

She let the girl direct her to a circle of pillows she'd placed around a box on the floor.

Settling on a cushion, Alexandra accepted a pretend teacup and sipped her make-believe tea. When she raised her hand to her lips, she caught sight of her wedding band and knew what she had to do.

Chapter Six

*T*he exterior of the Ministry of Health building had all the aspects of a prison, with imposing red-brick walls and tall, narrow windows. The building was meant to intimidate, but obvious neglect made it resemble a tired, aging behemoth rather than the guardian of health for the former Soviet populace.

Alexandra fingered the piece of paper in her pocket, her key into this bureaucracy, and gripped the packet of papers under her arm. She pulled hard on the heavy wooden door and entered a small anteroom, crossed it, and opened a lighter door to the Ministry's reception area.

As in most Russian buildings, the two sets of doors were designed to reduce heat loss. Not that it made much difference now. The city administration had yet to turn on the heat, and the building felt more like Siberia than the unusually sunny day outside.

Just inside the foyer, she hesitated. Those following her squeezed past with a scowl in her direction and flashed their credentials at the guard seated at an entry gate. Afterward, they proceeded through a turnstile toward a marble staircase beyond. Following their lead, she approached the guard and handed him the paper noting her appointment with the head of the Ministry's Maternal and Child Health division.

The guard examined the paper and grunted one word. "Passport."

After he studied the worn, red booklet identifying her as a citizen of the Russian Federation, he gave a raspy sigh and picked up a phone receiver. With a wave, he motioned for her to stand to the side to let others pass.

He mumbled into the phone and turned to her. "Wait here. Someone will come for you."

She clutched her file folder to her chest and observed the Muscovites as they moved in quick, purposeful steps. Matronly women in thick wool scarves and fur caps. Men in dark coats and short boots. Young women wearing imported clothing, their high-heeled boots clicking on the dull tile. Her own heavy coat and boots, so necessary for the Siberian winter, marked her as provincial.

To her relief, a small woman descended the stairs and stopped just on the other side of the turnstile. "Alexandra Alexandrieva Pavlova?" she asked. At Alexandra's nod, she responded, "Please follow me."

When she passed the guard, the woman glanced at her and asked, "Aren't you going to leave your coat?"

Only then did she recognize the cloakroom on the left. So anxious about the meeting, she'd forgotten to leave her things. Feeling even more like a serf, she shook her head. "No, I'm a little cold."

The woman gave her an odd look but turned to ascend the stairs. Alexandra followed her through a labyrinth of dark, wood-paneled corridors carpeted with Oriental runners until they stopped at one of the doors spaced along the wall. She stepped into a paneled room. A wooden table with two chairs with crimson upholstered seats sat in the middle of a Persian rug.

The woman pointed at the chairs. "Please wait here. Dr. Plitenskaya will arrive shortly."

The woman shut the door, leaving her alone. Alexandra placed her packet on the table and slipped her purse off her shoulder. After a moment, she took off her coat and immediately put it back on. The room was colder than the lobby, and she was grateful for not having checked it downstairs. She patted the packet with anticipation, thinking about all the effort it'd taken for her to get to this point. The number of people she'd begged to petition the Ministry on Nadezhda's behalf. The letters she'd written. The *svyazi* Yuri, his parents, and Vladimir had called in to do the same.

She touched the spot where her wedding band had been and shuddered, remembering the shouting match when Yuri learned about what she'd done.

When the door opened again, she jumped in her seat. A small woman with a halo of short, ginger-colored hair stepped into the room. Taking the woman's hand, she smiled into a pair of eyes set behind soft folds of flesh that gave the woman a sad-puppy appearance. After exchanging pleasantries, the woman took the chair opposite her at the table.

"Dr. Plitenskaya," she said, "I want to thank you for agreeing to meet with me."

"I could hardly refuse." The doctor smiled good-naturedly. "You have some very influential friends."

"The son of our delegate to the Parliament is a good friend. I have been most grateful for his help in this matter."

"Of course. Is that your daughter's file?" She pointed to the packet on the table. "May I?"

Alexandra pushed the folder across the table, and the doctor leafed slowly through its contents, stopping to examine one or another document. Her hands clasped together in her lap, Alexandra willed her patient expression to remain even as her heart drummed against her ribs.

When the doctor had finished, she turned the papers over so the regional hospital's latest report lay open in front for her. "The heart specialist recommended a transfer to the Cardiology Institute here in Moscow?"

"Yes. She had some treatment there, but the doctor said it was only temporary. He said they offer treatments at the Institute not available other places."

"She had pneumonia recently?" the doctor asked, holding up another piece of paper for more careful examination.

"Yes." She kept her voice steady despite the flood of memories of Nadezhda with needles protruding from her thin arms. "That's what they say weakened her heart."

"Is she here in Moscow now?"

"No. She's with her father, in Siberia. In Stop-100. We worry about her taking such a long trip."

"But she would be able to make the trip if she were admitted to the Institute?" she asked, folding her hands together over the papers on the tables.

"The doctor said she could with no problem."

Dr. Plitenskaya picked up another paper and held it up as if she were examining an X-ray. "According to this letter, your father was decorated for service to the country."

"He died in a laboratory explosion when I was young."

"And I see you and your husband worked at the same institute." She turned over the sheet and read the next. "Your supervisors praise your work. They describe your contributions as major advances in vaccine development."

Alexandra shifted in her seat. For so long she'd kept her work and Viru-Preparat secret, talking about it openly still made her uneasy. "I left after my daughter was born. We decided it wasn't wise for me to continue when we saw her condition. Unfortunately, leaving the Institute meant losing access to special health facilities."

"This comes to why you requested this interview."

"I have one more letter." She pulled a paper from her purse. Several stamps and seals marked the bottom of the missive, indicating various local and departmental clearances. "It provides additional information for admittance to the cardiology center."

The physician examined the letter. After a moment, she placed it on top of the other papers on the table. "Certainly all the paperwork is here, and your request is in order. I'll need to review everything with greater attention before making my decision."

When the doctor pushed back her chair, Alexandra's heart picked up speed again. The interview was already over?

She placed her hand over the other woman's. "Please, doctor. I appeal to you as a mother. My daughter's strong. When she was born, they said she wouldn't make it through the first week. The specialist in the regional hospital doubted she would survive her last visit there. The treatment here will save her life."

Dr. Plitenskaya stared at her. The folds around her eyes drooped further. She pinched the bridge of her nose. "I know you love your daughter, but you have to understand my position. I receive hundreds of requests like Nadezhda's every week. Some stronger candidates than her."

The woman gave a long, weary sigh. "We have only so much medicine, and must therefore select those who will benefit most. I've had to turn down children because of other defects that will make them a burden on their family or the State for the rest of their lives."

"Nadezhda's not like that, I assure you. She's not a burden. She's a blessing."

The doctor gave a brief smile. "Of course she is." She rose from the table and gathered the papers into the folder. Picking it up, she said, "I'll study these further and let you know our decision shortly."

Standing as well, Alexandra swallowed past the lump in her throat, seeking some sort of sign in the doctor's movements. Nothing. The physician opened the door to reveal the woman who'd escorted her to the interview standing outside. "Natasha Sergeyeva will see you out."

At the door, she gripped the woman's hand one last time. "Thank you, doctor. I'm staying with a friend. Her number's on the outside of the file. I look forward to your call."

This time the smile was perfunctory. "We'll be in contact."

Leaving the Ministry building in a daze, she passed the ride to Lena's apartment shifting from despair to fear to hope and back again as she examined and reexamined her brief encounter with Dr. Plitenskaya. One moment, she was certain Nadezhda would be accepted into the Cardiology Institute, and the next, certain the doctor would reject her, but hadn't wanted to appear hasty. By the time she reached Lena's apartment door, she'd decided Nadezhda's future came before all else, including Yuri, and she would take any means necessary to ensure it.

With a clear goal in mind, she felt lighter, as if a weight had been removed from her shoulders, and could even smile when Lena opened the door before she raised her hand to knock.

"What did she say?" her friend asked.

Once again, she was struck by her hostess's appearance. Always one of the prettiest girls during their school years, Lena had only improved after graduation. With easier access to fashions that complemented her tall, curvy frame, the woman had truly blossomed. For the third time that day, Alexandra's own appearance made her feel awkward, and her smile faded. "Let me get inside. What were you doing? Watching from the window?"

Lena stepped back to let her pass. "Are they admitting her?"

Alexandra shrugged out of her coat. "She said she would think about it."

"So she didn't say no."

"But she didn't say yes either."

"She will," she said with a hug. "Come into the kitchen and tell me all about it. I have *buterbrod* and water for tea."

"All right. Just let me call Yuri. I'm sure he's anxious to hear what the Ministry said."

Lena nodded and slipped into the small kitchen opposite the front door. Alexandra continued to the living room and slumped onto the couch, pulling the phone next to her. Her friend had rented a "Western apartment" from someone who'd remodeled in hopes of renting to a foreigner, only to learn foreigners wanted more than white walls and imported appliances. As Lena explained it, they also wanted to be near the city's center, not in one of its farout "sleeping districts." Desperate to recover their remodeling expenses, the owners had rented it at Russian rates.

Waiting for her call to go through, Alexandra smirked to herself. Despite the foreign phone's sleek design, the series of clicks and hums emanating from it were the same as those from a Russian one. Just like the apartment, below the surface lay the antiquated system dating back to the Revolution.

Yuri answered before the second ring. "Alexandra?"

She tried to read his mood from that one word. Anxious? Perhaps, but not angry. She gripped the receiver tightly. "How did you know it was me?"

"I calculated you would call two hours after your appointment. What did she say?"

"That she would review everything and be in touch." She twisted the phone cord about her finger. "Yuri…?"

What did she want to tell him? About her decision outside Lena's door? She'd no desire to start another argument across half a continent. What about her fears over the distance created by their last argument? Not something to be discussed over the phone. She sighed. "How's Nadezhda?"

"She's fine. You want to talk to her?"

"In a moment. Is she breathing well?"

"Don't worry. We have plenty of garlic around her room and her bed."

Was that all they had in common now? Garlic? She took a deep breath, deciding to try to bridge the gap between them. "I-I'm. I just wanted to repeat…how sorry…about what I said to you."

He didn't answer immediately. She listened for his breathing before speaking. "Yuri? Are you still there?"

He hesitated a moment more before saying, "I am too. Sorry, that is. Here's Nadezhda."

She bit her lip. Hardly the deep, soul-searching conversation she'd hoped for, but maybe it was all she could expect at the moment.

"Mommy?"

"How's my big girl?" she asked, forcing enthusiasm into her voice.

"I'm not big," she said, sounding exasperated. "Just a little bit big."

The smile came spontaneously. "How's my little-bit big girl, then?"

"Good. When are you coming home?"

"In a few days. I'm waiting to see if you can see a special doctor."

"So I can run and play like the other children?"

"You'd like that, wouldn't you?"

"A lot."

"Me too. Can I speak to Daddy?"

A moment later, Yuri spoke into the phone. "I'm going to put her down for her nap now."

"Yes, I'd better go. I don't want to owe Lena too much for the long-distance calls."

"How long will you be staying?"

"I don't know. I'll let you know as soon as they call."

He rang off before she could say more.

She sat on the couch with the receiver still to her ear until it gave off a harsh beeping. The noise pulled her from her thoughts, and she replaced the receiver. The call had the opposite effect of making her feel better. The chasm created by their fight seemed no smaller than before she'd left.

She joined Lena in the kitchen, slipping wearily onto a chair squeezed into one corner. The owners had painted its walls white too. She felt as if she were living the hospital again, only this time with better food. A plate of open-faced sandwiches of bread and cheese and two cups of tea sat in the middle of the table. After automatically dropping a few sugar cubes into one cup, she pulled it toward her. Lena offered the plate of sandwiches, but she shook her head. The knot that formed in her stomach during her conversation with Yuri would only allow liquids.

"How's Yuri?" Lena asked, taking a bite of one of the sandwiches.

"All right, I suppose."

She stared into her teacup, wishing she could read something in the leaves floating about. "He's changed so much. You remember what he used to be like in school? Happy. Caring. Lately, he's been so…bitter. I know he's worried about money. Who isn't these days? But you don't have to let it change you. We had a terrible fight just before I left and said some awful things to each other. I'm not sure it will ever be the same between us."

Lena put down her cup and leaned over to catch her gaze. "You think he'll divorce you?"

"I'm not sure I won't divorce him. I can't keep living this way."

"Do it," she said, straightening in her chair. "Do it. Divorce him. Come to Moscow and live with me."

Alexandra stared at her friend. "I-I can't — "

"You said you wanted to divorce him."

"I said if he continues like this. I just can't leave him…not now. What about Nadezhda? She's his daughter too. I can't separate them."

"Come and live with me anyway. I have enough room."

"And what would I do here?"

"Find a job, make money, live better than you would in that icebox of a province."

"But my friends. Yuri. His family — "

Her friend leaned back in her chair and smiled. "I knew you weren't serious about divorcing him."

"You deceitful little — "

"But I'm serious about the offer to come live with me. You speak English. Lots of foreign companies are hiring people who speak English. You're also young and pretty. You'd have no trouble finding a job."

She considered Lena's offer. Despite how bad things were between her and Yuri, she couldn't bring herself to think about divorce, but perhaps being apart a while…

She shook her head, shooing away such thoughts. "Not with

Nadezhda still so sick. Besides, it's not that easy to get permission to live in Moscow."

"Lots of people live here illegally. You just say you live somewhere close. It's easier to get permission to live in one of the neighboring cities. You could start looking for a job here while she's in the hospital."

"If it were so easy, everybody would be here. In addition to not having permission, everything I own is back there. I can't afford to bring it, and no one would buy it. I'm tied to Stop-100 just like a ship frozen in the ice above the Arctic Circle."

"But this is where all the jobs are."

"What kinds of jobs?" Alexandra asked, unable to keep the contempt out of her voice. "I'm a microbiologist, trained in one of the best schools. So were you, and you're working as a secretary. You should be giving orders, not taking them."

She immediately regretted attacking her friend and her job, but before she could say so, Lena laughed. "I never had your talent for the work. You were a natural. I'm sure you inherited it from your father. Just like Yuri and his father. Besides, I'm not working as a secretary just for the job. I'm doing it to meet foreigners."

Alexandra cocked one eyebrow.

"I'll tell you a secret, but you have to promise not to tell my mother."

Alexandra put her finger to her lips, and Lena leaned over her teacup.

"I came to Moscow to marry an American," she said, dropping her voice. "I'm getting out of this country. I'm tired of being poor. I want the things you see on TV these days. A car. A nice home. And a man who makes enough money for me to sit around and enjoy them. The company I work at has a lot of single Western men. I've been working on them, but most of them want to live here. They say it's better in Russia. Maybe for them. Certainly not for me. So I have another plan."

She raised herself tall in her chair. "I'm listed with a marriage firm. They're finding me a husband. That's how I'm able to afford this apartment."

"How does that help you with the rent?"

"I use them to get things. These men come here looking for Russian brides. We meet them at parties. I always pick out the richest looking one. If he likes me, I suggest we go somewhere for a few days so he can see Russia and get to know me better. We usually go to St. Petersburg, and I get him to buy me things."

"What kinds of things?"

"Clothes, mostly. Let me show you."

Lena led her to the bedroom on the other side of the apartment. Alexandra felt as if she'd entered Marie Antoinette's boudoir. A white, gold-gilded double bed with its two separate spreads dominated the room's center. To one side of the bed stood the wardrobe. On the other, a vanity table with mirror. Lena opened the wardrobe. Dresses crammed its small space. She pulled a blue frock from among many hanging there.

"I got this one from a businessman from California. He was short and bald — but so gentlemanly," she said, holding up the dress so her friend could admire its lines. "I'll share a trick with you. You need to look at their hands. They say a lot about a man."

"Such as?"

"If they are soft and well-groomed, a businessman. Also their fingers. Short, fat fingers mean…"

She wiggled her eyebrows, and Alexandra's cheeks burned when the meaning sank in. "Lena!"

"You have to know these things. They're important when choosing a husband. Also, I always ask if they have a gold card. That tells me how successful they are. So far, I haven't found one with both a gold card and long fingers, but I've had fun looking. I'm always kind to them when they suggest we continue corresponding. I explain we are just not matched, without Mentioning anything about fingers or gold cards." She put the dress back in the wardrobe. "I only keep the things I really like. The rest I sell to cover rent."

"That's it." Lena spun about and clapped her hands. "I have a way for you to make money."

"I can't go out with other men," Alexandra said, shaking her head so fast, her hair flew about her face. "No matter how difficult my relationship with Yuri."

"I'm not suggesting that. Although I still think you could find a husband if you ever wanted to. They have no problems with women with children. I've known several women who have children — sometimes more than one — who still found husbands. Of course you might have to settle for one with short fingers." The skin around her eyes wrinkled in amusement before her face became serious. "No, what I'm talking about is buying clothes and selling them back in the provinces. Lots of people do it. There are markets where they bring things from Turkey, Vietnam, places like that. People fill up bags with clothes and then go back to their village to sell them."

Alexandra considered the suggestion, her forehead creased with thought. "It might work in concept, but I can't. I told you, I sold my wedding ring to get here. How am I going to get the money to buy clothes?"

"I'll loan it to you."

"And what if I can't pay it back?"

"You bring back the clothes, and we'll sell them here when you come with Nadezhda."

"I have to try something," she said, a thoughtful slowness in her voice. "Yuri said we have to be creative, like Vladimir."

"This would be too small for Vladimir's tastes, but a good beginning for you."

"Every business has to start somewhere. Maybe this is mine."

"Then you agree?"

"I agree."

Lena hugged her. "Good. Tomorrow, we go to the market and begin your new career."

Before Alexandra could answer, the phone beside the bed rang.

Chapter Seven

$\mathcal{A}$lexandra sat at her kitchen table going over the old agenda she used as an account book. On one page, she kept track of the clothes she'd sold, which of her friends she'd let purchase on installments, and how much they owed. On another, she followed the prices and quantities of medications Nadezhda would need following her operation. The two columns were beginning to balance, but so slowly.

No sooner had she agreed to Lena's clothing idea than the Ministry called to say Nadezhda's operation had been scheduled. Now that she'd collected almost all of what her friends owed, she saw she needed to make more to cover Nadezhda's medicines. Vladimir had offered one more possible opportunity, but she feared Yuri's response to it.

She glanced about, seeking the peace she usually found in this spot. Like most Russians, she used the kitchen more than any other room. Perhaps the tradition went back to their peasant heritage when families huddled about the kitchen stove to keep warm. Unlike Lena's sterile, modern kitchen, artificial ivy decorated the ceiling's upper corners to give the space an out-of-doors feel even in darkest winter.

At the moment, she felt no such peace, but confronted many

worries. She examined the faded ivy without seeing it, leaned back, and rubbed her eyes. Her gaze shifted back to her account books and then to the plastic clock on the wall. Yuri still hadn't arrived home despite the hour. Where was he?

As if he'd read her mind, she heard him let himself into the apartment. He pushed open the kitchen's glass-paneled door, entered the room, and placed his hands on her shoulders. She stiffened at his touch, but he appeared not to notice, planting a kiss on the top of her head.

Leaning over her, he glanced at the book on the table and asked, "How's the clothing business?"

"All right." She tipped her head back to gaze up at him. "I've made back the money Lena loaned me. Once I get everyone to pay off what they owe, we should have enough to cover most of Nadezhda's medicine for the next year."

He opened the refrigerator and peered inside. "Is she sleeping?"

"I put her to bed several hours ago."

He pulled out a bottle of beer, popped open the top with the opener they kept tied to the refrigerator handle, and sat down across the table from her. She frowned as he took a long swig from the bottle. He stared back at her, his eyes flashing. "What? I can't drink in my own house?"

She shifted in her seat. Desperate to avoid another fight, she willed herself not to respond, but the words slipped out anyway. "Of course you can. You just seem to be doing a lot more of it than you used to. I smelled in on your breath when you kissed me. Where've you been?"

"Out," he said with a shrug.

"You spend a lot of time 'out.'"

The scowl on his face warned her she'd gone too far. "I don't have to answer to you. Or explain where I've been."

She massaged her temples. "No, but I waited for you. After two hours, I gave up and had dinner. You could've at least called."

"If you must know, I met up with Vladimir and some of his friends. The clothes you brought back from Moscow gave me an idea for making money. I'll admit I wasn't too happy with you when you showed up at the airport with two big bags."

"You yelled at me." The blood in her temples pounded harder with her recollection of the scene in the airport terminal.

"I thought you'd put us into more debt, but now I see what you're doing makes sense. People need clothes, and with the way you collect their payments — a little each week — they can buy them. You know what else they need? Car parts. One of Vladimir's friends works in a parts factory near here. The factory can't afford their salaries, so they pay them in parts. He'll sell them to me. I'll take them to Moscow and sell them there."

She tilted her head, seeing the potential in his proposal. On their way to the clothing market, Lena had told her about other markets for various products — electronics, CDs and movies, and even car parts.

"You could even buy more clothes there and bring them back here," she said. "It might actually work."

Her growing enthusiasm dropped when another thought formed. She squinted at him. "Where will you get the money to start?"

"I've thought about that too. I'll use the money you've made on the clothes."

"You can't. That's for Nadezhda's medicine. The Ministry of Health agreed to her operation, but you know they don't cover all her medication. We have to have the money for that — or her operation will be useless."

He glared at her over the beer bottle in his hand, his jaw muscles working. He'd set a similar face whenever he wanted her to do something she didn't think was right — like the day they'd skipped class to go to the movies with Vladimir.

"It's temporary. I'll make it back when I sell the parts in Moscow."

"It's too risky." Her features hardened to match his. "What if we lose the money? Where would Nadezhda be then?"

He stood, and his chair slammed against the wall behind him. "I can't believe you. You didn't worry when you borrowed money from Lena and bought all those clothes without even consulting me. Then you sold them to people on credit. On credit. With nothing but their word they would pay you."

"That was different." She forced her voice to remain calm to avoid another shouting match. "We didn't know how much Nadezhda's medicine would be. I wouldn't have risked it if I had. And the people who owe us money are our friends. We can trust them to pay us back. How well do you know Vladimir's connection?"

"You don't want me to succeed, do you? Even Vladimir says it's a good idea." He tramped about the space between the table and the refrigerator.

His reference to their friend opened the opportunity she'd been waiting for. She picked her words carefully. "Maybe you can use some of the clothes money. If we have a way to replace it. You know Vladimir's been pestering me again about working for him. What if I take the job after Nadezhda has her operation? And you could still buy your parts."

"No, damn it!" He pounded his fist on the kitchen table, making the account book jump. "I won't have you working. You're a mother now. Your place is at home."

"What's gotten into you?" she asked, her eyes wide.

"Ever since Nadezhda was born, you've been in charge. *You* stayed in the hospital with her through all the operations. *You* went to Moscow to petition the Ministry. *You* brought back the clothes and sold them. *You. You. You.* What have I been all this time? Your lackey. 'Yuri, get this medicine.' 'Yuri, she needs this. She needs that.' For the first time since she's been born, I have an opportunity, and you refuse to help."

Anger surged inside her, melting her resolve to avoid a fight. "How dare you?" She faced him. "I've done nothing but sacrifice for you and Nadezhda. All I want to do is to keep us together and healthy. Fine. Take the money I've been wringing from people and go buy your car parts. But I'm going to take the job with Vladimir. Your mother can look after her."

"You're going to abandon your daughter now?" His eyes formed two slits. "After all our work to make her well?"

"I'm not abandoning her. I'm making sure that she has the medicine she needs to live. You're the one who's abandoned us."

She'd hit a nerve. His face went slack, all tension draining from him. His voice had an eerie calm that frightened her more than his shouts. "It's not my fault I haven't been able to find another job. I've spent months looking. I've found something now — only you refuse to let me do it."

She dropped her voice as well, hoping he would see her logic. "I'm not refusing. I said to go ahead and do it. I just plan to make sure Nadezhda has what she needs."

The fire in his eyes flared, and with a spin, he stalked out of the kitchen. "Where're you going?" she asked.

At the kitchen door, he yelled over his shoulder, "Out. I'm going to let this man know you've given me permission to buy the parts."

Her stomach tightened. Even though he hadn't finished the beer, she knew with what he had before and the half bottle he'd had in the kitchen, if the police stopped him, they would arrest him for drinking and driving. Just the smell of alcohol on his breath would be enough to throw him in jail and confiscate the car.

"It's late," she said softly. "Do it tomorrow."

His hand on the kitchen door handle, he faced her. "You may be able to order Nadezhda around, but not me. I'm not a child. If I want to go out, I will."

"Please stay. It's not good for you to leave when you're this angry," she said, following him from the kitchen.

He forced his arms into his jacket. "Don't try to coax me like some child. I'm not in the mood to stay." After shoving on his boots, he jerked his gaze in her direction. "And don't wait up for me."

She crossed her arms. "Don't worry. I won't."

He slammed the door, and the noise woke Nadezhda. With the first startled cry, Alexandra ran to her bedroom to pick her up. Carrying the girl to her bed, she stretched out next to her to stroke the child's hair. Soon her daughter's tears subsided, and she fell back to sleep.

But Alexandra couldn't follow her example. She spent hours watching shadows from the streetlights dance across the ceiling. In her mind, she heard Lena's voice say with such confidence, "Divorce him" over and over again. Her friend had been joking, pushing her to make her see the love she still felt for him at the time. The thought keeping her awake that night, however, was whether her answer remained the same.

Chapter Eight

Sergei's footsteps echoed throughout his three-room Khrushchev apartment. When he and Svetlana had divorced two years ago, she'd demanded the apartment they had received when they married. He could have fought her for it because his position in the FSB had gotten them into the building, but the whole process had left him so numb, he hadn't cared who got what. Only after Svetlana had left his things in boxes in the building's hallway did he realize he was homeless. She had family she could've moved in with, but he had no one. He'd had to plead with her to keep his things until he found a place. Of course, his needs were simple. A room would have sufficed. He'd even thought about finding a place in a communal apartment with a single room and a shared kitchen and bath but quickly dismissed that idea. No one wanted to be around an FSB agent except other FSB agents. The stigma and fear of the KGB remained, despite the change in initials. Finally, someone desperate to leave town had rented to him, furniture and all, at a reasonable price.

And thus, his current living arrangements. Khrushchev's efforts to develop Russia had included the construction of five-story, walk-up buildings throughout the country. The structures, nicknamed *khutshchyoby* as a play on the leader's name and the word for slum, consisted of three-room apartments providing the most basic shelter. From the front door, he could see into all three rooms. Straight ahead, the narrow kitchen with barely enough space for two to stand side by side. To the left, the bedroom. Between the bedroom and kitchen, a bath and water closet. To the right, the living room. The furniture was all pure Soviet style, heavy with dark rough material. All in all, he mused, the perfect apartment for a solitary FSB agent.

He tossed his keys and the heavy folder he was carrying onto the coffee/ dining table in the living room. In the kitchen, he pulled a plate of *kalbasa* from the refrigerator door. After making quick work of peeling some potatoes, he fried the sausage up with the potatoes and a few slices of onion. As they sizzled, he helped himself to a shot of the vodka he kept in the freezer. Tossing it back, he let the icy liquid burn its way to his stomach.

Once his meal was cooked, he carried his plate and more vodka to the living room and sat down to review the papers he'd brought home with him. Something he couldn't have done while married. Svetlana had said more than once she hadn't minded marrying a FSB agent. After all, her father had been one. What she never tolerated was his bringing work home. Her father had never done that, she'd reminded him on a regular basis, and he'd held his tongue, never mentioning her father's career had also not advanced. He saw no use in explaining to her the difference between paper pushers who never went out of the building and agents such as himself. She'd had no interest in his job.

He flipped open the file folder Pavel had given him on his way home. Since the papers had never entered the FSB building, he hadn't broken any rules by detouring them to his house. The agency's politicians weren't going to learn about his latest effort until he was ready.

Although Pavel didn't have much aptitude for surveillance, Sergei had assigned him to follow the man Ahmed. He hoped Ahmed knew someone was watching him. His caution would only be more apparent, and given the details in Pavel's notes, it hadn't slowed down the foreigner at all.

The phone rang next to his elbow, making him jerk and toss the file's content onto the floor.

"Shit," he said as he cradled the receiver under his chin.

Marcus's voice drawled into his ear. "Well, hello to you too."

"I just dropped a file," he said and leaned over to pick up the papers and a stack of photos that had slid from the folder.

"Taking work home with you. A bad sign."

"Is that some American superstition?"

"No. It's a sign you don't have a life."

"Who's calling me at this hour about work? Maybe you're the one needing a life." He shuffled the photos into a stack and flipped through them. Sergei recognized most of them, local Mafia bosses and other denizens of Russia's burgeoning underworld.

"It's not quitting time yet in Moscow. Time difference, you know."

"Can I help you with something?"

"Just thought I'd check in. Find out what our man Ahmed is up to."

"He's been keeping busy," Sergei said nonchalantly. "You took my advice and been watching him?"

"Uh-huh."

"You're not going to share anything with me?"

"Not anything to share."

Marcus sighed into his ear. "Fine. You want anything from Moscow? I'll be in later for a meeting."

He surveyed his apartment and thought. Glancing at his dinner, an idea came to him. "Some fresh vegetables. Or fruit. Bananas. I'd like some bananas."

The idea of fresh fruit in this time of year in Siberia made his mouth water.

Marcus chuckled. "You find out what Ahmed's up to, and I'll bring you a whole bunch."

After hanging up the phone, Sergei took a sip of vodka and frowned. It was warm. He touched his dinner. It was cold. How long had he been talking to Marcus? He shrugged and took a bite of food. Chewing slowly, he studied the photos again. He stopped in midchew and picked up one for closer examination. A man in an imported suit and tie instead of the typical Mafia tracksuit was shaking Ahmed's hand. A smile crept across Sergei's face. Now he had an idea of what Ahmed was after. This file was definitely remaining at home for the time being.

Chapter Nine

Glancing up, Alexandra recognized Lena through the windows' layers of grime and peeling paint. The bus carrying Alexandra and Nadezhda from their plane to the terminal wheezed to a halt, and she grasped her daughter's hand firmly before joining the others pushing their way through the doors and onto the icy blacktop. Once inside the terminal, the passengers funneled through one small door where those waiting for the flight greeted them. Lena waved a bouquet of flowers as mother and daughter entered. Stepping to her, Alexandra accepted the roses, and Lena lifted Nadezhda for a hug.

The little girl shrieked at the stranger's sudden action and leaned backward in her arms. Lena quickly put her down, and Nadezhda ran to her mother's legs, hugging the nearest one tightly and burying her head in Alexandra's coat. She patted her on the head to comfort her, careful not to disturb the white net bow she had arranged on her ponytail.

"I can't believe how she's grown," Lena said. "And she's so beautiful. Like a little angel."

"You look well too. New coat?"

Lena turned to model the mink. "A Christmas gift from my fiancé."

"You're getting married? But it's only been two months since I left."

Before Lena could answer, the crowd rushed from the gate's exit toward the baggage claim area. Alexandra pulled her daughter from her leg and straddled the child on one hip.

As they entered the flow of passengers, she asked, "Why didn't you tell me?"

"Because I knew you were coming. I wanted to tell you in person." She stopped and turned to face Alexandra. Clasping her free arm, she said, "I finally found my American."

Reaching the group milling outside baggage claim, they waited for a purple-haired woman in an olive drab uniform to permit entry. Her stare warned everyone to stay back until the ground crew unloaded the baggage onto a cart behind a small tractor and chugged over to the terminal.

"Tell me about this man. From your coat, it's obvious he's rich — what else?"

"He's not rich. Just, as the Americans say, 'well-to-do.' He's not handsome, but not a toad like many. Most important, he's kind and gentle and polite. And so helpful. I had him to my apartment several times. He even helped with the dishes. He says he enjoys the way I dress. That American women don't know how to be feminine any more. They're more interested in proving themselves better than men. And they work so hard at it, they're turning into men. So, he loves to buy me things just so I look beautiful."

"The coat becomes you," Alexandra said. "When are you leaving for America?"

"As soon as we can work out all the details. The Americans are just as bureaucratic as our government. You can't imagine all the paperwork involved. We're going to get married here. I've started to plan it. You have to come," Lena said, grasping her free arm again.

Alexandra glanced at the little girl before replying. The child had an amazing talent for repeating the one thing no one thought she'd heard or understood at the most inopportune moment. Weighing her words, she said, "I'll see. Things are a little... unsettled for me right now."

Lena's eyebrows knitted together. "What's the matter? Something's bothering you."

"I'll tell you later," she said, shifting her gaze to Nadezhda.

Lena nodded and pointed to the tarmac. "Your bags are coming."

The matron opened the door to the baggage claim as an ancient conveyor belt creaked to life. The crowd squeezed through the opening to reassemble around the belt as a motley assortment of boxes, plaid plastic bags covered in tape, and dusty suitcases jerked past. Alexandra pulled two from the belt, and they joined the ragged exit line. The gatekeeper checked each passenger's claim tickets against those attached to the bag. After accepting Alexandra's tickets, the matron ripped the copies off their bags and waved the three of them through the door.

Once outside, Lena insisted on taking a taxi.

"My fiancé gave me a big allowance for the wedding. I can afford it," she said when her friend protested. "Besides, Nadezhda doesn't need a long bus and metro ride after that plane trip."

The driver appeared intent on setting some sort of speed record to Moscow, but despite the car's swaying and jerking, the child fell asleep in her mother's arms. Alexandra worried at how quickly her daughter tired. The operation had to be a success. Lena must've sensed her concern. She remained silent all the way to the apartment.

After leaving the bags and the sleeping girl in Lena's bedroom, the two women tiptoed to the kitchen. Two cups and saucers waited on the table, and Lena picked up a box of tea.

"You and Yuri still having problems?" Lena asked, dropping a teabag in each cup.

Alexandra sighed and slumped into a chair in front of one cup. "We argue about everything these days, mostly about money. Speaking of which, I have the money I owe you."

"Keep it," she said, pouring the water over the bags.

She opened her mouth to protest, but Lena raised her hand. "It's obvious you need it more than me. I'm about to marry my American and leave all this behind. The few rubles I loaned you are nothing to Fred. That's his name, Fred."

"Very American. You love him?"

Lena sat on the other side of the table and dunked her teabag. She rested her head on her other hand, a sheepish grin crossing her face.

"Yes." She giggled. "I know I sound like a schoolgirl, but I'm crazy about him. I can't explain it, but the moment I met him, I knew he was the one. Like you and Yuri."

Alexandra smiled to herself, remembering the day she realized she was in love with him. They were sharing a microscope in biology class. He had stepped back to let her peer into the eyepiece and given her a smile. Her heart had melted.

"It can't be exactly the same," Alexandra said, sipping her tea. "I knew him and Vladimir forever. A long time passed before I knew cared for him, but when I did…" She sighed. "I wish I knew what happened between us."

"Things aren't any better?"

Tears welled in her eyes. "Whatever I say makes him angry. If I ask him where he's been, he accuses me of controlling him. At the same time, he orders me about, telling me what I can and can't do."

"He was always so easygoing."

"There's no pleasing him now. Vladimir offered me a job, helping him with his business."

"Vladimir? I could see how Yuri might — "

"Don't say it. I've never felt anything for Vladimir. He only offered it out of friendship. I finally got Yuri to agree, but he keeps saying only until his own business gets started. He wants to be just like Vladimir. He's still competing with him, as if we were children in primary school. Do you remember how those two would compete for every prize the teachers offered?"

"Yuri would work so hard," Lena said with a nod. "Then Vladimir would get the prize. I think he charmed the teachers just like the girls."

"I'm not sure how much longer I can live like this. If it weren't for Nadezhda…"

"Come to Moscow," Lena urged, placing her hand over her friend's. "You can have my apartment when I move to America. I might even be able to get you my job."

"There's a part of me so willing to do what you offer," she said, touched by her friend's concern.

"You wouldn't even have to go back. Just stay here with me. Help me plan my wedding."

"I can't," she said, imagining her life as a single mother in Moscow. She pulled her hand from Lena's. "Who would look after Nadezhda while I worked? She'll need extra care after the operation, special medicines. Yuri's mother has already agreed to watch her so I can work for Vladimir."

"At least promise me you'll come back for my wedding. I'll pay your way."

"I can't promise. Not until after Nadezhda's operation."

"I know things will be all right. You just have to have faith. Look at me. Who knew I would find my American between your last visit and this?"

"So optimistic. Just like Vladimir. Maybe being around you and him will help my luck."

❧

There is no evil without good. Alexandra repeated the Russian proverb like a prayer. Nadezhda had survived the operation and would soon leave the hospital. But, as she listened to the surgeon, she wondered if the saying should be *there is no good without evil.*

The surgeon, tall, with short-cropped hair, and so thin his white coat hung on his frame, frowned, enhancing his ghoulish look. "You realize this operation doesn't resolve her problems. As she grows, so does her heart. Of course, since she has been admitted once, it will be possible to get her admitted later for additional procedures here."

"Will you be able to cover her costs?" she asked. "Like you did this time?"

"That's not something I decide. It's a pity. In the West, I've heard there are better procedures we don't offer here. If there were a way for you to go to the West..."

"In the West..."

"Your daughter has a chance of a normal life."

"How? Who?"

"I'll write down what I know, but I don't understand what you'll be able to do. As I said, it's not available here."

"I was able to get her here, into this Institute. I'll get her to the West. I have a friend moving to America. I'll start writing letters, asking for help, just as I did for this operation."

The man shook his head. "It's different over there."

"I have to try," she said. "If there's a way to cure her, I have to try."

Chapter Ten

Alexandra tapped on Vladimir's office door. Scrimping slightly on the reception area where she sat had allowed him to truly decorate his own office. The room reminded her of a museum painting. The carved Italian desk and upholstered chairs were heavy and dark. The building overlooked one of Stop-100's main streets, and just beyond the heavy, dark drapes and burglar bars, she could hear people and cars passing by. Several oil paintings decorated the flocked-wallpapered walls.

From the doorway, she could see him studying papers spread across the desk's veneered surface. One hand supported his forehead as he reviewed a column of figures scribbled on a pad in front of him. He smiled up at her and motioned her in. She handed him yet another stack of papers and waited for his response.

He flipped through them and gave her another smile.

"These look good. I trust they're in your usual impeccable English?"

"I don't know about impeccable, but definitely better than yours."

After he had signed them and handed them back to her, she remained in front of his desk.

"Is there something else?" he asked.

"I know I've only been working here a short time…"

"But…?"

"But I wondered if I could leave early today. I've done all the typing."

"Do you and Yuri have a special night planned?"

She felt her cheeks burning. These days, an evening without a fight was special.

"No, I want to go to the university library. I need to do some research." "Of course you can have some time off, but what are you researching?"

"I want to find out more about Nadezhda's condition." She pulled a slip of paper out of her pocket. "The surgeon told me there are procedures in the West they don't do here. I want to find out more. Then I start my next project, writing letters to get her to such a physician. I'll be asking for a letter from your father when I do."

"And he'll be happy to give it to you, like before. But you don't have to go to the university."

"I don't?"

"Use the Internet."

"Sergei, you know I can't afford to do that. I need my salary to buy medicines, not pay for time at some Internet café."

"Then use the one on your desk. I've wanted to show you how to use my account so you can send those letters from here. We'll start your first lesson."

"And I could send the letters I want to write, such as to the hospitals in America, through your account too? Please, show me how."

He walked with her to her desk in the outer office. She took her seat and shifted to one side so he could reach the keyboard. He clicked a few keys on the computer and an image formed on the screen. Cyrillic characters spelled out "Russia On-line."

"How did you do that?"

He typed some more and the screen went blank. "You click here, and then — "

He took her hand and placed it on the mouse. Putting his hand over hers, he guided her through the steps. The warmth of his hand together with her active search for Nadezhda's cure sent a thrill through her, and she could feel her cheeks warm.

"Because you speak English, this will be easier." He turned to her, his face inches from hers. She noticed he'd had wine with lunch.

"Now, what is it you wish to research?"

She handed him the piece of paper. He struggled to type the words while finding the right letters on the keyboard.

After he made several mistakes, she laughed. "Here, let me do it."

She moved even closer to him. His arms encircled her as she typed on the keyboard and he moved the mouse.

"You're much better at this than I am," he whispered in her ear.

Heat flooded her face again, but she quickly dismissed it as another image formed on the screen. Line after numbered line appeared.

"Read through these," he said, moving even closer to her.

She could feel his cheek touching her hair.

"And when you find information you want, you just click on it like this…and you will see more."

She held her breath as the image reformed once again. She frowned.

"This is no help," she said, scanning the screen. "There's nothing here about an operation."

"Well, you just go back."

She lost track of time. They continued going from one site to another, he leaning over her, his arms encircling her, teaching her new meanings to the words "address" and "page."

At one site, a broad smile broke across her face, and her eyes widened in delight. The answer glowed from the screen. She hugged him excitedly.

"This is it," she said. "Exactly what I needed. Everything, all in one place. And I found it in just a few moments. I could have spent days at the university library and still might not have found it."

She gave him a sheepish grin. "Now, how do I use your account to send mail?"

"I'll be so glad to have you do more of my e-mail. You can correspond with my contacts. I've gotten messages from them saying they didn't understand mine."

"You should've spent more time with your lessons instead of your teachers."

"It got me high marks. Besides, now I have you. Turn around and let me show you."

"And I'll be able to contact those who know about Nadezhda's condition?"

"If you have their address. Here, you start by…"

They spent a good portion of an hour composing and sending messages. The fifth one proved particularly difficult. She understood what he wanted to say, but finding the right words in English was difficult. He was leaning close to her again, reading over her shoulder. Intent upon the screen, they didn't hear the door open. They did, however, hear it slam closed. Yuri stood just inside the door strangling a bouquet of flowers. His face darkened to a furious crimson, and his eyes flashed black.

"Yuri, I can't believe you're here." She smiled broadly. "I have such wonderful news. Vladimir has been…"

"I can see what Vladimir's been doing," Yuri said.

Vladimir stepped from behind the desk. "Yuri, you misunderstand, we're only working. I was showing Alexandra — "

"It's pretty obvious what you were showing her," Yuri said. "I'm just surprised you call it 'work.'"

She stood, her anger matching his. "You have no right to accuse us of anything. He was helping me — us — find out about an operation for Nadezhda."

"I came to take you to dinner, but you're obviously engaged, 'working.'"

His gaze jerked to Vladimir. "And I thought you were my friend."

Vladimir raised his hands. "Yuri, wait. Please — "

"I'll let you get back to your 'work' and not disturb you further." He threw the flowers onto the floor in front of her desk, spun about, and stomped out the door. The reverberations from the slam echoed in the office.

"Do you want me to go after him?" Vladimir asked.

She tore her gaze from the door and cleared her throat.

"No," she said with a sigh. "He won't listen to you. He's not reasonable when he's in this mood. Give him time to cool off."

"I'll talk to him later." He smiled broadly at her. "Don't worry. I've always been able to get him to see things clearly. I've been able to talk him out of quite a bit of foolishness lately."

"What sort of foolishness?" she asked, worry coloring her words.

"Silly ideas about making money." He shrugged his shoulders.

"Don't get upset. I've convinced him about those, and I'll convince him about us."

He put his arm around her shoulder and kissed her cheek. "You have enough troubles. I'll take care of this one for you."

His arm remained draped around her shoulder, and she realized how long it had been since she'd felt comforted and protected. Hugging Yuri was often more like trying to embrace a hedgehog. At that moment, she became conscious of how far apart she and Yuri had drifted.

Chapter Eleven

Sergei once again lingered over a late-night supper in his living-cum-dining room and studied Pavel's latest report over his plate of sausages and potatoes. He found it convenient to meet the agent after work and keep his notes at home. Pavel was no longer following Ahmed. He was now learning more about the man from the photo — Vladimir Stefonovich Morozov.

The mere mention of this man made him frown. The Bureau had files on both Stefon Morozov and his son. Given the men's political connections, Sergei had to tread carefully. Accusing the younger Morozov of illegal activity would require strong evidence. Most politically connected people had some shady dealings in their background. Whatever Vladimir and Ahmed were developing together had to be important enough to bring to light. Otherwise, any charges would vanish just as they had against the Iranians, perhaps taking Sergei with them the next time.

He read Pavel's research on Morozov and son. Stefon Morozov had started the Trans-Siberian Trading Company after the Russian privatization spree of the 1990s. To shed itself of the country's industrial and commercial burden, Yeltsin's government had issued vouchers to every adult citizen to purchase shares in state companies earmarked for privatization. Many, however, saw no purpose in the process and preferred cash to some vague concept of ownership. Like others with a little more foresight,

Vladimir's father had obtained hundreds of vouchers from them, sometimes for only a small percentage of their face value. Using these vouchers and the support of other interested investors, the elder Morozov had purchased a large share in the company he'd managed during the Soviet period at a price much lower than its true worth.

After purchasing the company, he'd resold it to the company's original directors for a tidy profit. The senior Morozov had used his wealth to support his political ambitions and now served in the country's parliament. Actually, quite a clever move, that one. As a member of Parliament, he was exempt from criminal prosecution — one of the perks for Russia's elected officials.

Not so the son. But still, his father's success had supported his own financial dealings. Sergei sighed and sipped his vodka. It had warmed again. Scowling, he pulled himself off the couch and walked into the kitchen. After refilling the glass from the bottle in the freezer, he went back to Pavel's report. The Trans-Siberian Trading Company seemed much more impressive than its actual activity. Ostensibly, they specialized in importing products from the Middle East. Sergei grunted and made a note. Pavel hadn't indicated what products. He would have to talk to him about being more specific.

Morozov seemed quite busy. Pavel's report provided an extensive list of times, places, dates, and people met during his observations. Besides Ahmed, he met regularly with a number of local businessmen, most with mafia connections. Pavel's list included several descriptions with no names. Sergei made another note. He would need photos and names to go with these contacts. One of these might know something, and if the contact was more afraid of the FSB than the mafia, he might provide additional information. With such a target in sight, Sergei would take over from Pavel.

Chapter Twelve

*Y*our typing's getting faster," a voice behind Alexandra said.

She jumped, her fingers striking several keys at once. She hadn't heard Vladimir leave his office or come up behind her. "Yes, now I have to work on my accuracy."

She bit her lip, deleting the scattering of letters created when he had startled her. She could feel her cheeks growing hot. Ever since Yuri had surprised them the other day, she had tried to keep her distance from her boss.

As if he could read her thoughts, he asked, "Everything all right between you and Yuri?"

She shifted uncomfortably in her seat. She'd been able to convince Yuri she had only a working relationship with Vladimir, but in no manner were all things right between them.

"Yes," she said finally, "I think your reassurance helped as well."

"Good," he said quickly, checking the door and then returning his gaze to her.

Clearing his throat, he asked, "You never told him about that night, did you?"

She could feel the heat rising in her cheeks. "There's nothing to tell. Besides, it was years ago."

"He asked if we had ever…well, ever…"

She spun around in her chair, her eyes round. "What did you tell him?"

"That no, we'd never…that nothing ever happened between us."

"Good. Nothing did. I'd had too much to drink that night."

The night of their high school graduation, after toasting their success with champagne, they joined the whole class in touring the city — a time-honored Russian high-school tradition. Toward morning, she and Vladimir had gotten separated from the rest of the group. Trying to catch up with the others, they had tried a short cut through an alley. There in the darkness, Vladimir had pulled her toward him and kissed her. She had returned the kiss, and then another and another. Had a stray cat not knocked over some boxes and startled them, who knew where the kisses might have led? She had let down her reserve only that one time, and afterward, they promised each other to forget it. Obviously, neither had.

"We both had too much." He straightened his suit jacket. "I'm going out for a while. Call my cell if you need me."

"All right."

She busied herself about her desk as he put on his boots and coat and prepared to leave. As soon as he was gone, she saved the letter she'd been preparing for Vladimir and retrieved the one she had written to the US ambassador requesting his help to send Nadezhda to his country for her operation. As long as she kept up with her assignments, Vladimir didn't mind her using the computer for her own work.

Her presence was partly for show anyway. He really didn't have enough for her to do some days. He conducted most of his business outside the office over lunch or dinner or with his door shut. Although with her new ability to use e-mail and the Internet, she was doing more of his correspondence with those outside the country and even with banks, translating letters with references to shipments and cargo. He seemed to be making money. At least, he always paid her on time.

Just as she hit the key to save the letter, the door opened. She turned toward it, the smile on her face disappearing as soon as she recognized the person kicking off his boots in the doorway.

"Hello, Ahmed," she said in English, forcing herself to sound pleasant.

While he resembled someone from the Caucuses, the minute he opened his mouth, his accent marked him as a foreigner. She couldn't put her finger on it, but something about the man made her distrust him. Rather than ingratiating him to her, his charming manner made her wary.

"Is Vladimir in?" he asked.

"I'm sorry. You just missed him. I can call him on his cell," she said, reaching for her desk phone.

"I can do that. How is your daughter?"

"Fine, thank you. In fact, she is doing so well I'm going to Moscow in a few weeks for a friend's wedding."

"How interesting. Will you be gone long?"

"Just a few days."

"You will be missed. You make this office so much…" He looked thoughtfully at the ceiling. "How you say? Bright. You make the light here."

"Thank you," she said, suppressing a smile at his awkward English.

She turned back to the computer. "If you'll excuse me," she said, glancing over her shoulder, "I'm working on something."

She turned her attention to the computer screen and punched the keys to bring Vladimir's letter back on the screen. Out of the corner of her eye, she could see he hadn't moved to leave. Instead, he stood by the door, shifting from foot to foot.

"Is there something else?" she asked, now getting irritated at his interruption.

"Your husband. He is still selling car parts?"

"Yes. He's found quite a demand," she said. Actually, she was not sure about his business. She saw none of the money he said he was making.

"But he has no license, no?"

"His sales are so small he can't afford one. Besides, he says the police aren't interested in such a small enterprise."

"He should really have some protection. I could help him find some. It is very dangerous to be without a roof," he said, using the Russian slang term for mafia. "They would make sure he has no problem with the police."

His not-so-subtle reference to protection money made her shift uneasily in her chair. She forced a smile and said, "I'll pass your offer on to him."

"You tell him I have powerful friends — better than Vladimir's. They can protect him."

"I'll tell him."

"Goodbye." He smiled and gave a slight bow. "I will look for Vladimir now."

"Goodbye," she said and turned to the computer, keeping the smile on her face until after he had shut the door behind him.

She stared blankly at the screen, unable to concentrate now. His remarks made her pulse skip wildly as she examined all their short conversation signified. That he knew Yuri was selling car parts was disconcerting. She had never mentioned it to him, even though he was in and out of Vladimir's office all the time. She didn't like telling the man anything. Her intuition told her the more he knew, the more dangerous he could be. So, besides knowing Yuri sold car parts, he also knew he had no license. Another dangerous bit of information.

But the most dangerous of all, the one that made her heart pound, was his reference to a roof.

She had worked for Vladimir long enough to understand how the mafia worked here. Vladimir had his own connections. Several times a month, two burly men in tracksuits and short-cropped hair paid him a visit. After a brief chat, he would give them an envelope, and they would leave. She always held her breath while they were there. The papers reported daily on bombings and fires at businesses failing to pay enough or paying to the wrong group. She feared they would pull out something and toss it into the office, blowing them up. Or worse, shoot them both. The papers carried even more stories about assassinations of local businessmen. They never mentioned the secretary being killed, but she couldn't be sure the death of a secretary would have been newsworthy.

She had once asked Vladimir if it didn't bother him to have to pay these thugs, but his response was to raise his hands in a sign of helplessness and say, "It's just part of the cost of doing business."

She shuddered, thinking about such men becoming interested in Yuri's little business. Vladimir might be able to afford to pay off these men and include it as part of business, but she was pretty certain Yuri couldn't.

❧

She waited up for Yuri that night and repeated her concerns to him. They were seated at the kitchen table, talking in low voices so as not to disturb Nadezhda.

"You should be more careful and not draw attention to

yourself," she said in conclusion.

"Don't be such an old lady. Things are going well. In fact, I'm thinking about expanding. If I do, you should quit your job."

"I don't think I should," she said, shaking her head. "There are still Nadezhda's medicines to buy…"

"I'll be able to take care of that. You're my wife. If I think you should quit, then you quit," he said.

She sighed. She could tell he was readying for an argument, but she couldn't let his remark go. He would only interpret her silence as acquiescence.

"And I have no say in the matter? What if I like working? What if I don't want to quit?"

"You're still my wife," he said, his volume rising.

"Meaning I'm just supposed to obey you?" she whispered back, fighting the urge to raise her voice as well. "I always thought we had a partnership."

"We do. I take care of the money, and you take care of the home," he said in a low whisper.

"Since when?" she asked, not caring now if her voice grew louder. "I can't believe this. You once told me you were proud of my degree and job."

His voice matched hers. "That was when the job was at the Institute, not as a secretary."

"Well, you're sneaking around selling car parts from the trunk of a car."

"That's going to change. A few more times, and I'm going to be able to afford my license."

"If you don't get caught first."

She drew in her breath. What had she said? To voice such a thing out loud was sure to make it come true.

"Maybe you'd like that just so you could keep working for Vladimir?" His expression hardened. "That's it, isn't it? You like working for him, don't you? Don't forget I saw you that day."

Blinking back the tears his words brought, she softened her tone. "I already explained that to you. If it's truly important to you, I'll quit."

His jaw muscles tightened as his mouth formed a thin line. Rising from the table, he said, "I've told you, you can't cajole me as if I were an infant. Damn right you're going to quit and because I said so. I'm going out. Don't wait up."

"Don't worry. I won't. I've learned how to spend a pleasant evening alone without you."

He opened his mouth, then shut it, as if he had decided against whatever he had wanted to add. With quick strides, he left, shutting the door solidly behind him. As soon as he was gone, she spit over her shoulder three times and sent a prayer to heaven in the hopes of warding off the evil she had conjured. The last thing he needed now was trouble with the mafia…or worse.

Down the hallway, Nadezhda cried out for her. The door slam must have awakened her. Alexandra rushed to the bedroom and picked her up. Cradling her, she whispered to her to hush. The child wrapped her arms about her neck, and her sobs subsided into whimpers. She turned to place her daughter back in bed.

"No," the girl said, raising her head. "Please, Mommy. Can't I sleep with you and Daddy?"

"Daddy went out, but I would like that very much."

Carrying her to their bedroom, the two lay down on the bed. As Nadezhda's breathing slowed to the rhythmic pattern of a deep sleep, Alexandra's own tears began to slip down her cheeks. She wanted so much to believe Yuri knew best, but his view of reality didn't seem to match hers. She knew the numbers from her account books. She couldn't quit yet. If she got responses to her letters, got Nadezhda to the West and her operation, she would have to quit, but not yet — no matter what Yuri thought.

She must have fallen asleep at some point because a soft pat on her arm woke her in the morning. Yuri sat on the edge of the bed. She stretched, causing Nadezhda to stir, but not waken.

"I'm sorry," he whispered and held out a bouquet of flowers.

She smiled and accepted his peace offering, sniffing their mild fragrance.

"You were out all night?"

"I stayed at Vladimir's. I was so angry last night, but I really didn't have a place to go. I walked around a little while then went to his place. I was lucky. He was alone and let me stay. We spent most of the night talking. He convinced me that I was being foolish and that I should let you keep your job."

"If it makes you uncomfortable, I won't. I could look for another…"

He shook his head. "It's wrong of me to object to your working or being around Vladimir. Our mothers worked, and it didn't hurt us. And Vladimir assured me I just misunderstood things. I guess I'm just frustrated that I can't provide for you and Nadezhda as I should."

"You're trying. I know that. Times are hard."

"Anyway, he convinced me he needed you and I was being selfish. I may have been a little jealous that you've been able to help Nadezhda more than me. That's going to change when I get my license. I promise you, things will be different."

He leaned over and kissed her deeply. Nadezhda stirred again and opened her eyes. She smiled up at her father and reached out to him. He picked her up and the three hugged.

"When you get back from Moscow, things will change," he said, meeting her gaze over their daughter's shoulder.

Chapter Thirteen

Alexandra watched Lena lift the champagne flute to her lips and stare lovingly into her new American husband's eyes. She was wearing a cloud of white lace and net. The skirt billowed wide about her feet and the tight bodice with two wings of net off her shoulders accentuated her thin waist and smooth shoulders. Fred, her husband, dressed in a tuxedo and wearing a sash crosswise across his chest, appeared dashing, despite his rather squat, plain figure. Alexei, the group's unofficial photographer, snapped a series of pictures of the happy couple in front of Russia's monument to their victory over fascism in Moscow's Victory Park.

The park, southwest of Moscow's center, attracted more than its share of sightseers, wedding parties, and families enjoying the bright February day. The ground's rolling hills stretched for kilometers along on the city's major arteries and offered the perfect place for sledding. Parents pulled tightly bundled children in small sleds resembling lounge chairs. Older children in snow suits and knit caps zoomed down the hills on contraptions resembling tricycles with skis. Youths and adults carried cross-country skis and poles on their shoulders, seeking the perfect flat area.

As soon as Alexei lowered his camera, Lena said, "Quick, give me my coat. I'm freezing!"

Alexandra rushed to her friend's side and draped the mink over her shoulders, taking care not to crush the dress's net wings.

"What possessed me to decide to marry in the middle of winter?" she asked, stamping her white slippers against the frozen cobbles. "This has to be the most ridiculous tradition we have in this country — riding around, drinking champagne, and getting your picture taken outside in the cold."

"What's she complaining about?" Fred asked Alexandra, his unofficial translator.

"That I'm cold," Lena translated herself. "It's a silly tradition to spend the day outside taking pictures when we could be in a warm apartment, drinking hot tea and vodka."

"I kind of like it," Fred said, taking in the huge monument of Russia's patron St. George slaying the dragon of fascism. "It's the first time I've seen some of these places."

"It's much easier on you than me. You have on a suit at least. Try doing this without anything on your arms."

"Your wish is my command," he said with a bow.

He pulled off his tuxedo jacket and flourished it about like a matador's cape. After swinging it over his head, he tossed it to one of their group.

"Are you crazy?" Lena asked. "You'll catch pneumonia."

"Perhaps," he drew her close and kissed her lips. "But at least I'll have a beautiful woman to nurse me back to health."

The wedding party applauded, and Alexei snapped a few more pictures of them in their impromptu embrace.

"You see," Lena told her friends in Russian, "that's why I married him. He does everything I ask him to."

"What did you say?" he asked again.

"That you are a good husband." Alexandra winked at Lena.

"Now put on your coat before you freeze and let's get back in the cars," Lena said and turned to her friends. "Where shall we go next?"

"The university?" asked one.

"Yes. By the river," Alexei said. "It'll make a brilliant shot."

"All right, the university," she said. "Maybe I'll buy a fur hat for Fred while we're there."

The group trooped back to their line of black cars. A strip of ribbons down the center of the hood and trunk decorated each car, indicating they were with a wedding party. The lead car, which transported the wedding couple, carried both the ribbons and a plastic double ring on top.

A short while later, the cars pulled into parking spaces in front of the lookout over the Moscow River. Behind them stretched a long lawn, divided in two by a fountain dropping in levels from the sprawling, castle-like Moscow State University to the road. A red granite banister at the back of the outlook kept sightseers from falling down the embankment. Across the river, the city's center spread out to the north. On the right, a ski-jump sloped through the trees toward the river.

Slamming car doors and laughing merrily, the group reassembled on one side of the ski-jump. This took some effort because they had to squeeze past a long line of vendors set up along the walk. Alexei, with Lena's fur coat draped over his shoulders, ordered the group into various positions and snapped away, first with the river in the background and then with the imposing university behind them.

As soon as Alexei had snapped the last shot, Lena complained about the cold again and demanded her coat back. They handed out the glasses for another toast to the couple.

Alexandra was beginning to feel the alcohol and decided from the group's boisterous spirit that the others were as well. Their laughter grew louder as they browsed the vendors' tables. She wandered away from the group, who watched as Fred tried on various fur hats. She studied the cityscape below her. Cranes poked their pointed noses above the gray metal rooftops and bare treetops below, indicating another new building was under construction. No wonder everyone talked of going to Moscow. It offered a vitality missing out in the provinces. She could see it just in the short drive they had made from the park to the university. Where she lived, both people and city were just getting by. Holes pockmarked the roads; water and electricity would disappear for hours, sometimes days, without warning; even the people appeared ragged and gray.

She wondered if Lena's offer of her apartment was still open. Perhaps she could convince Yuri to come to Moscow with her. After their row over his license, he had tried to be more attentive. In response, she had raised the idea of resigning with Vladimir, explaining how she planned to quit once Yuri legitimized his business. To her surprise, Vladimir had not protested too greatly, perhaps understanding her need to work on the marriage.

Living and working in Moscow would offer them both a fresh

start. Yuri could sell auto parts in Moscow just as well as in Siberia. Better, perhaps. There were more cars in the capital. As for herself, despite her earlier contempt for Lena's job, she, too, had become a secretary. With such experience, she probably could find a job. She wanted so much to talk with Lena, but hadn't found the time. She needed to hurry before her friend left for America.

Her in-laws, of course, would be a problem. They were all the family both she and Yuri had left and were devoted to Nadezhda. She couldn't see how they could leave them in Stop-100. At the same time, they were no more able to move than the rest who continued there because they had nowhere else to go.

She shook her head. Such thoughts were a pipe dream. Her only true goal was to get Nadezhda to the US.

She sighed and wandered over to a table displaying wooden toys. She picked up one with a round, wooden paddle holding a bear. A string attached to the bear's arm hung below the paddle, weighted down by a wooden ball. By moving the paddle and making the ball swing, the bear's arm moved up and down as if he were ice fishing through a hole in the middle of the paddle. She smiled, thinking about how much Nadezhda would like it. Seeing the children in sleds at the park had made her realize how much she missed her.

"How much?" she asked the vendor, a man in a dirty fur hat and two days' growth of beard.

He stamped his feet and tossed aside the stub of a cigarette. "Forty rubles." She could smell the vodka on his breath. She gave the toy one more turn and watched the bear ice fish some more.

"Twenty."

"Consider the craftsmanship," the man said in an offended tone. "Thirty-five."

"Twenty-five, my final offer," she said, fishing the bills out of her purse and flashing them at the man.

"All right, but you're robbing me." He sighed and took the money from her.

He produced a rumpled plastic bag from his pocket and placed the toy inside. By the time he handed the bag to her, Lena and the others were calling from the parking lot for her to hurry and join them.

They drove around the city some more, visiting more sights, drinking more champagne, and posing for more photos. By the time they returned to Lena's apartment to continue the party, the sun was already setting.

Lena had hired someone to prepare a typical Russian banquet with caviar, potato salad, smoked salmon, and herring with beets. Additional bottles of imported champagne and vodka also waited for them. They had pulled the kitchen table out to the living room and borrowed a few more tables to create one long, narrow table stretching across the room. Bowls of food lined its center. The group gathered around and filled their plates and glasses.

Lena had insisted Alexandra sit on one side of Fred to continue translating for him. Trying to explain the long, elaborate speeches each guest made when it was his or her turn to toast the happy couple taxed her language abilities and energy, especially after a few more glasses of champagne. The men made a point of draining their vodka glasses to the bottom each time. After she explained to Fred it was a display of honor, he tried to match their efforts by doing the same.

At one point in the evening during a lag in the speeches, he turned to her and asked in a rather slurred voice, "You're from Siberia?"

"Yes, Lena and I grew up there together. She left. I stayed."

"Ah, the town with no name, only a number," he said, turning in his chair to face her fully.

"Yes. It's what you Americans called a secret city."

"Stop-100. What does that mean?"

"The train station was one hundred kilometers from the regional center. People simply used that to name the stop. I used to work in a biomedical research center there. I'm a microbiologist."

"I thought Lena told me you worked as a secretary."

"I do now, after I left Viru-Preparat," she said, swirling her champagne glass and watching the bubbles chase each other to the top.

"Times are hard there just as they are everywhere in Russia, huh?"

"It's definitely worse in the regions than in Moscow," she said. "Everything in town was there because of the research center. With so few jobs now, most people are unemployed these days."

"I remember reading about something that happened in one plant out there in Siberia, a while ago. Something about some chemical escaping and killing some people."

"Not a chemical. A disease. Anthrax. It wasn't where we lived. It was in a bigger city, Yekaterinburg."

"Weren't you scared, working in a place like that?"

She started to respond, but before she could answer him, someone stood and announced the next toast. She translated the wishes of happiness, joy, and future prosperity for the couple, and they drained their glasses again.

After completing all the toasts, someone struck up a Russian folk song, and they all joined in. She was glad they had chosen a happy one. With all the champagne and vodka, they would all have been sobbing if it had been sad, and it had to be bad luck to cry on your wedding day. They were making so much noise she didn't hear the phone ring and was taken by surprise when someone motioned to her she had a call. She squeezed out of her chair and pushed past everyone to get to the kitchen and the phone.

"Hello," she said.

The voice on the other end sounded familiar, but she couldn't understand the words over the singing at the table.

Plugging one ear with her finger, she made out Vladimir's voice. Her smile faded and her face drained as his words became clear. With all the chairs in the other room, she had nowhere to sit but on the floor. Sinking to the cold tiles, the phone still pressed to her ear, she held onto the cord as if it were a lifeline.

"Yes, of course, I'll be back tonight," she said.

She had to repeat it. Vladimir had not heard her whisper the first time.

After he rang off, she continued sitting on the floor. Only the blast of a busy signal in her ear brought her thoughts back to the kitchen. Pulling on the phone cord, she rose from the floor with shaking legs. She replaced the receiver without seeing it and stumbled back to the party.

Her ashen face stopped the singing.

"I need…" She tried to swallow, but found her mouth dry. "I need someone to take me to the airport. I have to go."

One of men who had chauffeured the cars about town that day stood. "I can take you. I still have the car and haven't been drinking."

"My plane leaves at midnight. I'm going into the bedroom to change and pack my bag. I'll be out in a few minutes."

She turned as if in a trance and moved out of the room. She

could hear the guests buzzing behind her back. Or at least she thought it was the guests. Her ears could still be ringing. Once in the bedroom, she placed her bag on the bed and put in the first few items with shaking hands.

She glanced up when Lena entered the room and shut the door behind her.

"What is it? What happened? Is Nadezhda all right?"

"Nadezhda is fine. It's Yuri. He's been arrested."

She picked up a piece of clothing and as if on autopilot, placed it neatly into the small suitcase.

Chapter Fourteen

Alexandra stared out of the airplane window at the snow-covered ground passing beneath her. The sun was just coming up and objects below cast long, thin shadows through the reflected light. That's how she felt. All frozen, stiff, drawn out. She hadn't slept all night. She'd replayed her conversation with Ahmed, the fight she'd had with Yuri, and her unintended curse. Following that, she'd tried to develop a plan for dealing with Yuri's predicament. Would her savings for Nadezhda's medicines cover the lawyers, fines, and other related costs? She tried to estimate how long what was stored under the floorboard in their bedroom would stretch.

Just as the plane began its descent, she finally drifted off to sleep. In her dreams, she flew over the snow-covered ground, feeling the cold air on her face and arms. She jerked awake when the other passengers applauded as the plane touched down. Immediately after the plane's final bounce, they jumped from their seats to retrieve whatever they had stowed overhead.

After waiting for her row's turn to disembark, she joined the ant-like march down the exit ramp and shuffle-slide along the icy asphalt to the terminal. She let the crowd push her through the narrow opening into the building. Vladimir waved at her from the other side of the arrival gate.

He took her bag from her hand and hugged her tightly.

"Don't worry," he said when he released her. "I'm taking care of everything. It'll be fine."

He looked down at her bag in his hand. "Is this it? Do we need to go inside for another bag?"

She shook her head. "No, that's it. It's good of you to pick me up, but where's Yuri?"

He cleared his throat and glanced away from her. Pointing in the direction of the parking lot, he said, "Let's talk about it on the ride to town."

His arm around her shoulders, she allowed him to lead her to the car. She wanted to lie down and sleep forever, never waking up or having to face what lay ahead.

"What exactly happened?" she asked, once out of the lot and on the road into town. "I could barely hear you when you called."

"There's not much to tell." He shrugged. "Yuri called me at home yesterday afternoon. The police had stopped him on a routine inspection. They saw all the car parts he had in the back and asked what he was doing with them. I guess they thought he had stolen them. When he said he was going to sell them, they asked to see his merchant's license. When he couldn't produce it, they arrested him and confiscated his car and the parts."

"Where is he now? In jail?"

"No, I was able to get him out last night. He was so upset and embarrassed, he didn't want to go home or come to the airport. He's at my place. Nadezhda's with his parents."

She watched the birch trees lining the roadway blur past. Snow frosted their trunks, and ice sparkled on the branches. After a moment, she asked, "Why do you think the police stopped him? I mean, how did they know he had something in his car?"

"From what I could tell, they just stopped him. You know how they are. They just point their stick at you, and you stop."

She sighed again. She knew the scenario so well. The GAI, the traffic police, in their heavy gray coats and big white cuffs staked out heavily traveled roads, especially toward the end of the month if they hadn't yet made their ticket quota. If they caught a violator, they pointed their black-and-white-striped stick at the passing car. The driver was required to stop and provide his registration and license. If all the papers weren't in order, it contributed to the officer's required monthly quota of tickets.

She couldn't let go of the idea that more was behind Yuri's

arrest than met the eye. "But why yesterday? When he had the parts in his car?"

His next remark made her recall the unintentional curse she had placed upon her husband and cringe. "Just bad luck I guess."

They rode the rest of the way in silence, and after a short time, she dozed off, only to wake with a start when the car pulled to a halt in front of his apartment building.

She let him help her out. Her whole body ached from tension and lack of sleep. She moved stiffly up the stairs of his building. At his apartment door, she leaned against the frame while he opened it and then entered ahead of him.

She called out for Yuri, but received no answer. Thinking he might be asleep, she headed to the bedroom. She had just opened the door after lightly tapping on it when she heard Vladimir's anguished cry.

She ran back toward the front and found him standing in the now-opened door to the kitchen. She only caught a glimpse of the kitchen before he pushed her back toward the living room. What she saw made her put her hand to her mouth and her stomach churn. He pushed her onto the couch, and she closed her eyes to keep from vomiting. The image of Yuri's feet dangling about shoulder height in front of Vladimir flashed across her mind. She shook her head, trying to erase the image.

Vladimir shook her shoulders and called to her. She opened her eyes. His face swam in front of her. She couldn't focus, but his voice came through the fog. "Stay here," he said. "Don't get up."

She rocked back and forth, covering her ears with her hands to block out the noises coming from the next room. She heard him curse loudly as he pulled open a drawer. He must have pulled too hard, making its contents clatter onto the linoleum floor. He screamed insults and obscenities between grunts of physical exertion. A dull thud echoed through the room, and she knew he had cut Yuri down. He threatened and pleaded with Yuri to breathe.

After what seemed an eternity to her, silence. Her ears rang from the heavy quiet settling on the apartment. Hearing his steps toward the living room, she squeezed her eyes shut and pressed her hands into her ears, refusing to let enter what she knew was coming. The couch shifted as he sat down heavily next to her. Drawing in one shaky breath, she released all the torment and despair in the sob that followed. He pulled her to his chest and let her wail against it.

When her sobs subsided, he cleared his throat. "He left this," he said, holding out a folded piece of paper with her name on the outside. "I found it in his pocket."

She opened the paper.

"I'm sorry," it read.

She turned a tear-stained face to him. "Sorry? Sorry! For what? For taking his life? For getting arrested? What kind of an explanation is that?"

"I had no idea he was so depressed. I should've never left him alone." He shook his head. "I'll take care of…of the…of Yuri. A doctor must come to examine him and declare him…He has to come. Then probably the police. I'll take care of it. I'm going to take you to your house. There's no reason for you to be here. I picked you up from the airport and took you home. We didn't come here."

She continued to stare at the piece of paper. Crumpling it in her hand, she spoke to the middle of the room.

"Oh, Yuri…Yuri…We would've worked it out. I know…"

He grabbed her by her shoulders and shook her. Her head snapped back and forth like a rag doll's. Her gaze focused on his face, and she concentrated on what he was saying.

"Did you hear me? You weren't here. I took you to your house from the airport. Say it."

"I wasn't here," she repeated. "You picked me up from the airport and took me to my house."

"Good. Now come on."

He helped her up from the couch and with his arm around her, led her to the front door. As they passed the kitchen, Alexandra turned for a glimpse, but Vladimir had shut the door. She could just make out a shape on the floor through the patterned glass. He shoved her roughly away from the scene and out of his apartment.

❧

The next few days became a surreal dream to Alexandra. She was aware of everyone gathering at her apartment — Yuri's parents, Vladimir, her friends — speaking in low voices, clucking their tongues and shaking their heads sadly. They cried with her, patted her on her hands or head, and murmured words of condolence, shock, and surprise. Day and night lost meaning to her. Once, she got up from bed and started to make breakfast. Her mother-in-law came into the kitchen, her hair sticking out at funny angles and her cotton bathrobe tied under her heavy bosom, and scolded her for making such racket at three in the morning.

Somehow, she managed to endure Yuri's funeral. The heavy odor of old incense, dust, and wax brought back memories of other funerals. Her father's, celebrated so long ago and with no coffin, only his picture in a frame for the priest to bless. Her mother's, held so recently. The reminder of her losses made her ache inside. She desperately wanted to bury her head in her mother's shoulder and cry. Instead, she had to be Nadezhda's rock when she tried to explain her father wouldn't be seeing her again.

The flickering candlelight cast elongated shadows that danced on the icon-covered walls as the priest intoned prayer after prayer in Old Russian. At one point, someone led her to stand beside the coffin. She gazed at Yuri's peaceful face under the white cloth they had put on his forehead. She bent down and kissed him lightly on his cheek. As she lifted her head from the coffin, she realized she was clutching Nadezhda's hand in hers. She reached down and lifted her daughter so she, too, could view her father. Following her mother's lead, Nadezhda bent down from her mother's arms and kissed him one last time.

Vladimir had arranged it all — the coffin, the priest, the ride to the cemetery, the plot, everything.

That night, following the funeral, Alexandra felt as if she were awakening from a nightmare. The people who had come and gone and filled the apartment with hushed voices and the scents of cooking food receded. Her in-laws were still sleeping on the couch, but she no longer felt invaded and intruded on by others. She sought out Nadezhda. Gently, she gathered her from her bedroom and brought her to lie next to her in her own bed.

The girl stirred slightly but settled back to sleep in her arms.

Alexandra held her and spoke in a quiet voice. "When I was just your age, I first met your father. I don't remember the day exactly, just that we always seemed to be together, in the sandbox, on the swings. And Vladimir too. How we'd laugh. And sing. Your father knew the words to all sorts of songs."

She stroked her hair. The girl snuggled closer to her.

"And then one day, I gazed into his eyes and knew...just

knew…he was more to me than a friend. My heart nearly burst if he came near me. I was so afraid he just saw me as a friend. Finally, I asked Vladimir to find out how he felt about me. I floated home the day he told me Yuri felt the same way about me."

Tears fell on the sheets and covers.

"Now, he's gone. At first, I thought my heart would break this time for sure. But I'll survive — for you — and we'll carry him in our hearts."

She kissed her daughter's hair and pulling her closer, fell into the first peaceful sleep she'd had in days.

Chapter Fifteen

Sergei gave an annoyed "come in" in response to the knock on his office door.

Yevgeny had given him some meaningless paper assignment. He was tired of doing the man's work for him. Glancing up and seeing Pavel standing in the doorway, shifting from one foot to the other like some eager puppy, only increased his irritation. He wore his blond hair longer than most and always seemed in a nervous hurry.

Sergei waved him into his office and motioned him to close the door.

"I told you I preferred to pick up your reports on the way home."

Pavel checked behind himself, as if the door he'd shut suddenly sprouted ears. He leaned forward and whispered, "I know, but I didn't think it should wait."

Sergei's gaze shot to his face. "What is it?"

"There was a death in Morozov's apartment yesterday." Sergei leaned back in his chair. "A friend of his hanged himself while Vladimir was out. At least that's what Vladimir told the police."

"You don't believe him?"

"Yes and no. That's why I wanted to share the news with you right away. The man was his friend, and he had stayed with him the night before, but a woman was there too."

"During the night?"

"No. She came in the morning. She's his wife."

"Vladimir's not married."

"No, I mean the wife of the dead man. Vladimir left. Brought back the woman, then left with the woman and came back alone. The police arrived, and that's how I know the man hanged himself."

Pavel gave him a quick, self-satisfied smile.

Sergei put the tips of his fingers together, forming an inverted "V" with his hands. After a moment, he asked, "Do you think Vladimir killed this man, or did he and the wife do it together?"

"Oh, they did it together."

"And why do you think that?"

"I've seen these two together before. She works for him." "Do you have the coroner's report?"

"No," Pavel replied slowly.

"So you have no information on the time of death or any other forensics for this conclusion?"

Pavel dropped his head, making Sergei feel guilty. He regretted being so hard on him. He could see his potential and wanted to nurture it. After all, Pavel had been pulling a lot of extra duty for him, probably ignoring his wife, and he knew only too well where that could lead.

He gave him a smile and softened his tone. "We just need more information. See what the coroner says, get copies of the police report, and find out more about this man and his wife. It may be just as it appears, or there may be more of a story as you suspect."

Pavel straightened his back, and Sergei could see him resist the urge to salute him. "Yes, sir."

Turning on his heel, he fairly marched out the door.

Once alone, Sergei tried to concentrate on the work on his desk, but found his mind returning to Pavel's news. The key here might be the woman. They seemed easier to turn. If she worked for Vladimir, she would be privy to more than even a wife might.

He leaned back and smiled. He would have to wait for Pavel to provide the official information before he made any final decisions, but it might be time for him to take over from Pavel, or at least give him a break and let him spend some evenings at home with his family.

Chapter Sixteen

*T*wo days after the funeral, Alexandra stood outside Vladimir's apartment door. She raised her hand to knock, then let it drop to her side. Taking a deep breath, she raised her hand again and rapped sharply. After getting no response, she rang the bell beside it. She could hear his heavy footfall approaching the door. Several locks clicked, and Vladimir's face appeared in the crack.

"Alexandra. I wasn't expecting to see you here. Just a moment."

He closed the door. She could hear him moving about the apartment, and then he reopened the door. "Come in."

She accepted his hug after entering. They stood just inside the apartment. She glanced past him and saw the doorway to the kitchen. Suppressing a shudder, she turned to put it out of her line of sight. In doing so, she noticed he had closed the door to his bedroom.

"How are you doing?" he asked, placing a hand on her shoulder.

"All right," she said. "I wanted to thank you for all your help. The police, the funeral, everything…I'm afraid I was in such shock, I never thanked you."

He shook his head. "There's no need. I was glad to help. In some ways, I feel responsible. If only I hadn't left him alone…"

"Please, we had no way of knowing." She glanced down at the parquet floor and then up at him. "I've come to see when you wanted me to come back to work. I know I talked to you about quitting, but that was before Yuri… Before Yuri died."

"Are you sure that's what you want?" He held her at arm's length and studied her face carefully. "It's only been a few days."

She lifted her hands in a sign of resignation. "Nadezhda and I have to eat. Besides, I can't stand to stay in the house. Everywhere I look, I see Yuri's things. I see them, and I-I — " Tears welled in her eyes. She blinked them back angrily. Meeting his gaze, she said, "I'll go mad if I stay at home."

His hands still rested on her shoulders, and he gave them a brief squeeze.

"Of course you can come back. What about Nadezhda? Where's she now?"

"With Yuri's parents. They're all the family we have left, and she's good therapy for them. They feel closer to Yuri with her around — at least that's what they say."

"When do you want to start?"

"Tomorrow, if it's all right with you."

"Let's say the day after tomorrow," he said after a moment. "I don't have much work right now."

"Day after tomorrow," she said, nodding. "I guess that would be best. I need to go to the police and see about the car parts. And the car. You said they confiscated both, and I've got to get them back. I need to return the parts to the man who gave them to Yuri to sell. Otherwise, I have to pay him. And I could sell the car."

He frowned. "I doubt you'll have any luck. They took him to the central *militzia* office. The car and parts might be there, but they could be anywhere, or nowhere. You want me to come along? I could go with you tomorrow."

"No," she said after a brief hesitation. "I'd rather try myself. I'll let you know if I need help."

"All right. Please, see me if you have any problems."

"Of course."

He hugged her once again — this time a little longer — and kissed her on the cheek. She gave him a weak smile and turned toward the door. She pulled the door open and ran straight into Ahmed. She recoiled, stepping back into the apartment.

He pulled his chin back and shifted his gaze from her to Vladimir before breaking into a smile. "What a surprise to see you."

"She was just leaving," Vladimir said.

Ahmed handed Vladimir his long, black leather coat "A pity. How are you doing, my dear?"

"All right," she said quickly.

"I'm very sorry about your husband. He was a good man, just…unlucky."

She bit her lip to keep it from trembling. "Yes. I guess so."

"Is everything all right?" He studied her curiously. "You are rather…how you say? Upset?"

"Just tired, I guess," she said, pushing past him toward the door. "I have to go. I'm in a hurry. See you later, Vladimir."

She pulled the door shut behind her with a shaking hand. She knew her actions were rude, but the thought didn't bother her. An uneasy feeling still possessed her about Ahmed. She had no evidence, but considered him somehow involved in Yuri's death. It seemed too coincidental Ahmed warned her about the license one day, and shortly after, the police arrested Yuri for not having one. That was the other reason for her to go to the police. She had to find out who turned him in.

◈

The *militzia* office was located in one of the drab government office buildings in the center of town. Built to impress all who entered it, it loomed tall with dark windows hiding secrets within. Long accustomed to disdainful treatment by petty officials, she waited just within the doorway by the guarded reception desk for an eternity. At long last, a man in a rumpled, ill-fitting suit appeared and called her name. He introduced himself as Capitan Nimrov and ordered her to follow him. After a series of dim hallways, they arrived at a small office outfitted with a scarred desk, ancient file cabinets and a straight-back chair. Nimrov gestured to the chair in front of the desk and seated himself in a cracked leather chair on the other side. File folders decorated every part of the office. They made towers on the desk, sat in awkward angles on the cabinets, and lined the walls. Some carried a layer of dust, attesting to the *militzia's* diligent attention to many of the crimes committed over the years.

"How can I help you, Alexandra Alexandrieva?" he asked.

He pulled open a desk drawer and removed a packet of cigarettes. He held the packet toward her. After she refused his offer, he shook a cigarette out for himself and stuck it in his mouth.

"I understand the police confiscated some items when they arrested my husband. I would like them back."

His chair gave a wrenching squeak as he leaned forward and blew a cloud of blue smoke into the air. Resting his forearms on his desk, he shook his head at her. "Sorry. Can't be done. They're evidence."

"Evidence for what?" Her eyes widened with disbelief. "My husband's dead."

He raised his shoulders and took another puff. "They're still evidence. We can't release them to you or anybody."

"My husband received those parts on consignment. He was going to pay it back when he sold — "

"Illegally sold. Your husband didn't have a trade license. I have the file right here," he said, patting a brown folder on the top of a pile on his desk. He picked it up and opened it, turning over several papers with small, cramped writing covering them.

Her fingers itched to review the papers, to see what they contained. They *had* to hold the answers to so many questions.

As if he could read her thoughts, the man picked up the file and put it in his lap, giving her an odd look. He selected one sheet of paper and held it just below the level of the desk.

"Says right here he confessed. Didn't even deny he had no license. The evidence can't be released."

"May I see the file? Where's this evidence being held?"

"No." Nimrov placed the paper back in the file and shut the folder sharply, gripping it in his hand as if it would fly to her if he didn't restrain it. "It's confidential."

"Can you at least tell me how you knew he might have the parts in the car?"

His eyes formed two slits. "That's confidential also."

The cigarette smoke floating between them nauseated her.

"Exactly what can you tell me?"

"Nothing," he said sharply. "I can tell you nothing, show you nothing, give you nothing."

"But surely the case is closed? My husband's dead."

"Perhaps." He smiled sympathetically. "But all information is confidential. I would suggest you forget the whole incident and go on with your life."

Her mouth dropped open. "I can't just 'go on with my life.'

My husband left debts others are demanding I repay. Factory workers paid in car parts who need the money or the parts back. I have neither. Surely you understand why I need them back? It's the only way I can end this debt."

"I appreciate your situation, but it's impossible for you to get them back," he said, a sharpness entering his voice.

She leaned back in her chair as the reality hit her. "You don't have them, do you? You, or someone else, took them. Probably sold them yourselves."

The officer rose from behind the desk, his face darkening. "What you're suggesting is illegal and unethical. Unless you have some proof of your accusation, I would suggest you keep your thoughts to yourself. It's not wise to throw about such charges without proof. Go home. Forget about this. There's nothing more for me to tell you."

He strode from behind the desk, opened the door, and gestured with his arm for her to leave. She rose slowly from the chair, straightening herself to her full height. She stared him in the eye. "I will find out what happened to my husband. I can't forget about this. I have a child to raise and need the money for her."

"Then for the sake of your child, forget about this."

He raised his hand. She flinched, expecting a blow. Instead, he gestured to a young man dressed in a similar ill-fitting suit seated in a common work area beyond Nimrov's office door. The man stood, ready to escort her out of the building. After giving Nimrov one last pleading glance, to which he did not respond, she headed toward her escort. She heard the officer firmly close his door behind her. Following the young man through the building's labyrinth, all she could see was Nimrov's hand clutching Yuri's file.

❧

On the bus ride back to her apartment, she considered her options. She could press to see the file and possibly find out who tipped off the police and what happened to the car parts; she could once again turn to Vladimir and ask for his help in the matter; or she could heed the officer's warning and forget the whole matter. Forgetting the matter didn't appeal to her. Yuri had killed himself from the shame of the whole incident. She couldn't possibly give up, in memory of him and his honor.

She was so deep in thought that she didn't notice the two large, black cars parked in front of her apartment building. Neither did she later recall anything out of the ordinary in the building's hallways or her front door. She was taken totally by surprise when she opened her door and found three men in suits seated in her living room. They had helped themselves to her meager supply of vodka, and had obviously been there for some time. The bottle was almost empty.

She started to run from the apartment, but one of the men roughly grabbed her arm and dragged her back into the room. Tugging her arm from the man's grasp, she said, "Get out of my home."

The most elegantly dressed one, who had seated himself in the middle of her sofa, gestured to an empty armchair. She glanced at it but remained where she was. The man who had grabbed her took her arm again and pushed her into the chair.

"Now, now, Slava, show some respect," the man in the middle said. He turned to her. "You'll have to excuse him. He's used to dealing with some of the less desirable elements in our society."

He picked up the bottle from the table and offered her a drink.

"No thank you," she said stiffly.

"Allow me to introduce myself. My name's Nikolai Kamovski. Perhaps your husband mentioned me?"

"He tended to keep his business to himself."

"Pity, because I'm afraid he owes me a rather substantial sum."

"Stand in line. He left debts several places."

"Perhaps. But I'm only interested in the one he left with me."

"You've come to the wrong person. I have no way to pay you or anyone else back."

Nikolai leaned back on the couch and studied her for a moment. She glared back at him.

"A most unfortunate situation. I'm a businessman, you see, and I have to make money or I'm out of business. I have a reputation to maintain. What about the others to whom I extend credit? Should they hear I let off one debtor, they might feel they deserve similar treatment."

"I told you, I have no money. Look around you. Do you see anything worth what he owes you? If so, feel free to take it. Otherwise, get out."

He scanned the room with an air of contempt. She knew how little he'd value the modest items she and Yuri had so carefully purchased. Finally, his gaze settled on her. She shifted uneasily in the chair as he examined her. He picked up his vodka glass and took a sip. The light glinted off the diamond ring he wore on his little finger. He settled back in his seat and crossed his hands on his corpulent stomach.

"There may be another way to pay his debts. I am, after all, a businessman with many different interests. You speak English, don't you, Alexandra Alexandrieva?"

"What of it?"

"As I said, I have many interests. One of which is the casino your husband visited on a frequent basis. I am always in need of young women to assist the customers. You could work there."

He leaned forward and studied her again. "Yes, you would work out well there. I have a business proposition for you. The casino's not very big, but this is a small city. All the same, we often have foreign guests there. I understand you can speak English. You could work off your husband's debt there."

"What would you expect me to do?"

"Nothing illegal…or immoral. I could use you as a hostess or waitress. You would serve drinks, show guests to their tables, duties such as that. Of course, should you wish to work out some separate arrangements with some of the guests for additional entertain-ment— "

"I'm afraid you have the wrong woman." She rose from her seat. "I'm not interested in that kind of work."

The man stood as well. His gaze traveled over her once again. "Pity. You would do well there. If you're not interested in such a solution, then I'll simply have to ask you for the money."

"I told you I don't have it. I'm trying to see if I can get the items the police confiscated from my husband. If I can get them back, I could sell them and then pay you back."

The man waved his hand. His ring glinted as he did so. "I'm afraid it wouldn't be enough. You see, your husband had quite a few gambling debts."

She drew in her breath. Gambling? Yuri?

"I can see your husband didn't tell you much about his pastimes. The wives always seem to be the last to know. I will leave you with my offer of employment at my casino. Think about it.

You have two days. Come up with the money, or go to work for me. Good day."

He dropped his business card on the coffee table and moved toward the door. The two thugs fell in line behind him. Before leaving, he turned. "Two days. I promise you. With your looks, you could pay off your husband's debt in no time."

After he exited the room, Alexandra rushed to the door and bolted it shut. When she returned to the living room, she sat down and picked up a small, framed picture of her and Yuri on their wedding day. Tears filled her eyes as she remembered how happy, how full of hope, she had been that day.

"Oh, Yuri," she whispered, running her finger over the glass. "What happened? Is all this what you meant by 'I'm sorry?' How could you leave me like this?"

Her finger traced his face, and she felt his smile mocking her. Anger coursed through her.

"Coward," she said and threw the photo across the room.

The sound of glass breaking against the wall filled her with satisfaction. She swiped the tears off her face and went to the closet to put on her coat again. She'd promised to pick up Nadezhda from her mother-in-law. After that, she would sit down and decide how to solve her problems.

Chapter Seventeen

Sergei rolled down his car window and dropped a banana peel onto the street. He'd have to ask Marcus to bring some more the next time he came. He had just enough time to duck behind a day-old copy of Pravda after rolling up the window when someone opened the door to the woman's apartment building. He sat on the passenger side of his car, pretending to wait for the driver to return from one of the buildings bordering a courtyard filled with dilapidated playground equipment, corrugated metal garages, and shards of glass.

The apartments had been built in the seventies or eighties. The Soviet Ministry of Housing approved only a few designs every decade or so, making establishing the time of construction straightforward. These particular buildings were twenty stories tall and one apartment deep, making them long, flat buildings of prefabricated concrete. Tiles covered the outside walls, punctuated with doorways leading to common stairwells.

He had followed the woman here after she left Morozov's apartment. His instinct had told him to — one of the few skills he couldn't teach Pavel. He just knew she would provide more information on this case than if he kept observing Morozov.

And his instinct had proved right once again. He instantly

recognized the man in the middle of a group of heavy-set men exiting the building. What did a low-level mafia boss like Nikolai Kamovski have to do with this woman? Of course, Pavel had already provided him with a great deal of information on her, but this contact with Kamovski offered a new wrinkle.

The mafia boss's cars ground over the snow and onto the street. Sergei dropped his newspaper, losing himself in thought. He could mentally envision his growing files on Morozov and acquaintances. He opened the one with Alexandra's name and reviewed the papers contained there. First, he remembered her picture, taken from her official file at the Institute. Young, pretty, yet something in her eyes. A sadness, perhaps? He knew all about the daughter. They had copies of most of the letters she had written petitioning for help.

He pulled up his newspaper again. She was leaving. Waiting until she turned the corner, he slid over to the driver's side and put the car in gear. He kept the bus she took in sight as he drove an acceptable distance behind in traffic. Pavel had some new work to do.

Chapter Eighteen

Vladimir said nothing, simply listened intently, his hands pressed together as if he were praying, while Alexandra summarized the previous day's events. She sat on the other side of his office desk, her fingers twisting around each other.

"I hate to come to you again with my problems," she said, "but I don't know what else to do. You've got the connections to get me a copy of the file. I have to find out who turned Yuri in to the police. I'm also hoping you can help me come to an arrangement with this Nikolai. Maybe on weekly installments, as I earn it here…"

He now leaned forward, resting his elbows on his desk. "You know I'll always help you. Really, it's not a bother to me. I'm just not sure what I can do in the first case. Let me call some of my *militzia* contacts. I probably can't get a copy of the file, but may be able to find out if it mentions any names and if the parts are still there. Like you said, they're most likely gone. Already sold. Forget about them. Let Yuri rest in peace."

She rose from the chair and paced in front of the desk. "I can't. I used up most of Nadezhda's medication money to pay the workers back." She stopped suddenly and turned to him. "Besides, I have to know if somebody betrayed him. Not knowing is making me crazy."

He rose from his chair and moved to her side of the desk.

When he placed his hands on her shoulders, she felt tears well in her eyes.

"Don't worry," he said. "I'll try my best to find out about Yuri. As for Nikolai, I know him. Not well, but enough. He's true mafia and into everything — gambling, extortion, prostitution. But he's also a businessman. We'll work out some sort of arrangement to pay off Yuri's debts. I don't have enough cash at the moment, but once my new project with Ahmed is done, I can pay him in full. In the meantime, we'll get new locks for your doors."

She hugged him. "You're too kind. I promise to pay you back. I'll work for you for free."

When he returned her hug, a new sense of gratitude washed over her. Without him, she hated to think of her fate. The night before, she'd spent a sleepless night trying to solve these new problems. She feared she might need to join the "night butterflies" who populated the streets after dark. She'd seen them, lined up in the glare of a car's headlights, stamping their feet to keep warm as their madam negotiated with a car's driver. Once again she cursed Yuri for leaving her to even contemplate such a fate. Now, in Vladimir's arms, she turned over these new problems to him as she had when Yuri died.

He relaxed his embrace and tipped her face to gaze into her eyes. "You don't have to work for free. There's still Nadezhda to worry about. But I do need your help — tonight, in fact."

"Tonight? But Nadezhda — "

He placed a finger on her lips to silence her. "Ahmed and I are meeting with the clients for our new venture tonight. I'll need an interpreter."

"I'd have to ask my mother-in-law to keep Nadezhda all night after she had her all day. She's always so tired at the end of the day. Besides, I'm not a real interpreter. You need a professional — "

He placed his finger on her lips again, gave her a wink, and returned to his side of the desk. After dialing, he sat down and rocked slowly in his chair. "Hello, Katerina Borisovna."

His casual tone with her mother-in-law let her know he considered the woman already under his spell. "How are you…? Yes, we don't talk very often any more…I have a favor to ask of you. I need Alexandra to work late tonight. It's very important for me. Would you mind letting Nadezhda stay the night? I promise to let her have the day off tomorrow to make up for it."

He nodded slightly, listening to Yuri's mother chatter. Finally, he replied,

"Thank you very much, Katerina Borisovna. We'll get together soon."

He replaced the receiver and smiled at her. "Your mother-in-law has agreed to care for Nadezhda tonight. All night. We won't have to worry about the time. A meeting like this could go on for quite a while."

"All right, Vladimir," she said, resignation tingeing her voice. "I'll go out with you and Ahmed tonight."

"It's strictly business. I promise. In the meantime, let me show you what needs to be done."

She followed him back to her desk, and he rattled off a list of documents needing to be typed and letters needing translation. At the back of her mind, however, was the gnawing realization of how quickly and deeply indebted to him she'd become. Had Yuri felt as overwhelmed as she?

Chapter Nineteen

$\mathcal{V}$ladimir sent her home early to get ready for the business meeting.

"Go home and change," he'd said. "You'll need an evening dress for tonight. Be back here by seven."

The light was out on her apartment's landing, but tenants were always stealing the bulbs — a trick left over from Soviet times. Her hand was in her purse, searching for her keys, when a man materialized beside her. She'd heard nothing, merely became aware of his presence beside her. She flinched, dropped her keys, and bolted toward the stairs. The man picked up her keys and grabbed her arm in one fluid movement.

"Don't run off, Alexandra Alexandrieva. You won't get very far without these," he said in a low voice.

He straightened himself and dangled the ring from one finger in front of her face. His slight smile suggested her attempt to get away amused rather than annoyed him. "Besides, I'm not going to hurt you."

"I thought you were someone else," she said, glancing down at the hand still on her arm.

He let go.

"Your acquaintance Kamovski, perhaps? Or maybe Ahmed, Vladimir's friend?"

She squinted at him, trying to make out his features in the hallway's half-light. "Who are you?"

"So rude of me. Borisov, Sergei Andreivich, at your service," he said, giving a short bow. "I work for the FSB."

She swallowed hard, trying to keep her face still and hide her shock. The KGB by any name still made her stomach jerk in fear. "I've done nothing." Her level voice didn't betray her racing heart. "What interest would federal security have in me?"

"We've been watching you for a while."

"You've mistaken me for someone else."

"Pavlova, Alexandra Alexandrieva. Born August 16. Widow of Yuri Ivanovich Pavlov. Daughter, Nadezhda Yuriyevna Pavlova, currently spending the night with her grandparents. Shall I continue? We do have the right person. You caught our eye some time ago. As soon as you left your job at the Institute."

"That was several years ago. Any information I have would be of no use to anyone."

"We're not interested in what you used to do. We already know that. We're interested in what you're doing now."

"Typing letters? I'm afraid that's rather boring."

A sound from a floor below made the man cock his head. Footsteps clicked on the tile floor and echoed in the stairwell as their owner descended the stairs. "Perhaps we should continue this discussion inside?"

"I have nothing to share with the FSB."

"Did you know your friends Vladimir and Ahmed have been seen recently in the company of an Iranian?"

"And?"

"No one has asked you about your work at the vaccine lab?"

"No."

"As you can tell, Alexandra Alexandrieva, we know a lot about you and your family. I can assure you we plan to keep our eye on you."

"The FSB must have nothing to do these days if you're following me around."

"Your father died in service to his country. We want to make sure you don't dishonor his memory."

"I've done nothing to dishonor him. And I resent the implication I have or would."

"We want to make sure you continue his memory. We're here to make certain the Motherland he so unselfishly served remains for the future. You do care about the future, if nothing else, for your child?" His voice lifted at the end, and his gaze met hers, challenging her to deny either her love for her country or her daughter.

The reference to Nadezhda sent another stab of fear through her. She raised her chin and glared at him. "I'm more interested in the present. Helping her survive for now. I have to work tonight. If you'll excuse me, I must get ready."

She turned to put her key in the door, blocking his view of her trembling hand. The man reached around her. For a moment she feared he was going to arrest her. She wouldn't be the first citizen to merely disappear thanks to the KBG.

Instead, he placed his hand over hers, and spoke into her ear like a lover. "There's nothing I can do to convince you I'm sincere?"

A spark of anger ignited within her and rose to heat her cheeks. How dare he touch her? Talk to her in such an intimate fashion? She spun about to face him. "All right. Prove yourself. Someone betrayed my husband to the police. Tell me whose name is in his file, and we'll talk."

"Are you sure you want to know? You might not like the answer."

"I'm certain. If you want my help, tell me who killed my husband. Because whoever gave his name to the police killed him as surely as if he'd put the noose about his neck."

He gave another short bow. "As you wish. We'll meet again later." He held out his hand. "My card. In case you change your mind and wish to talk."

"I doubt it," she said, grabbing it from him. Anything to make him leave.

Without glancing back, she turned to the door and stepped inside. Once safe in her apartment, she locked it loudly and vowed to change them all the next day. She listened for his footfalls on the landing, and only when she heard them echo down the stairs did she let out a long, slow breath. What in the world had brought her to the attention of the FSB?

Chapter Twenty

Sergei couldn't help but smile to himself. Leaving the rabbit's apartment building, he knew she'd turn. She'd shown some rebellion, but all the signs were there. First, she feared him. She'd tried to hide it, and he admired her efforts to do so. But the daughter was the key. A mother's love always served as an excellent motivation for betrayal. He had seen women spill secrets on their lovers, parents, even husbands, in return for their children's protection.

He respected that. A much nobler motivation than greed. He'd often been able to get what he needed for just a few rubles, or playing on someone's need for revenge. A lioness's fight for her cubs was righteous anger. Second only to loyalty to the Motherland. He had known too many who'd given their lives to defend Russia for him not to list patriotism as the most honorable incentive.

He walked back to his car to wait for her to leave. She'd not brought her daughter home as she usually did. Something was afoot, and she would lead him to the answer. No need for him to seek out the *militzia* for the answer to her question. He already knew who turned Yuri over to the police

Chapter Twenty-One

Alexandra tried not to stare at the man Ahmed escorted into the office, but he was hardly the person she'd imagined as Vladimir's business contact. Ahmed held the door for a man with a full, dark beard. Once inside, Ahmed helped his guest out of his coat. The man wore a dark suit, the white shirt underneath buttoned to the collar with no tie.

"Good evening," she said in English and extended her hand. "I'll be accompanying you as your interpreter."

The man glanced at her hand and gave her a deep bow without taking it.

"This is Mohammad Dehghani," Ahmed said. "He is with an Iranian company. His English is not so good. So I will speak to him, and you speak to me."

"That could be confusing. Wouldn't a Russian interpreter who speaks Farsi be better?"

"For business, yes. But this is pleasure. A pretty girl is much better for pleasure."

She hesitated for a moment then smiled. "Yes, of course. Let me see if Vladimir is ready. Would you like to take a seat?"

The men settled into the two armchairs set to one side of the outer office, and she rapped quietly on Vladimir's door. After entering, she took a spot in front of his desk and crossed her arms.

"Ahmed and his friend are here. He says this is not a business meeting."

"He's just confused." He waved his hand dismissively. "We

have to show this man a good time. Entertaining is part of doing business. I need someone to help serve as hostess. You've always been good at that, much better than I am."

He cocked his head to the side and smiled. "That dress is lovely, by the way."

She smiled back, knowing he was charming her, but accepting it. "I've had this for years. I'm glad it still fits." She sighed. "I guess it's a little late for you to get another interpreter."

"Besides, you need a night out. It'll be good for you. Let's go."

She opened her mouth, briefly considering mentioning her visit from the FSB agent. She shut it just as quickly, remembering the agent's knowledge of Nadezhda and her whereabouts. What if he decided to arrest her in-laws instead? The KGB wouldn't have hesitated.

Vladimir followed her into the front office, putting on his most jovial face and immediately charming Mr. Dehghani. After elaborate greetings and a brief discussion about cars and drivers, they walked outside and split into two groups. Ahmed and Dehghani went to a chauffeured car; she and Vladimir followed in his black Mercedes.

Their short drive carried her into a world she'd only glimpsed through her association with Vladimir — the life of the New Russian. The restaurant was located in a recently constructed Western-style hotel built to accommodate foreign visitors to the region. The lobby shone with bright lights, sparkling floors, and chrome fixtures. Elegantly set tables of crystal, china, and stiff linen greeted patrons sporting imported clothing, gold watches, and cell phones.

As soon as a tall, pretty girl left them with their menus, Alexandra immediately began to earn her money, translating and explaining the various dishes and following the conversation going on around her.

Vladimir insisted on imported vodka to start. The price took her breath away. At first Mr. Dehghani declined a drink, stating it was against his religion, but after some coaxing from both Vladimir and Ahmed, he took a few sips. In true Russian tradition, Vladimir drained his glass with each toast.

The drinking and toasting continued throughout the meal and long afterward. They raised their glasses to the impending sale between Vladimir and Mr. Dehghani, Ahmed's assistance to the process, the health of all involved, and so on. Despite their insistence she join them, she declined, explaining she needed to stay sober to translate and drive home. Never once did they clearly express the nature of the transaction, and that suited her. After the visit from the FSB agent, she decided the less she knew, the better.

They remained at their table until the staff informed them they were closing. Mr. Dehghani took his leave at that point, simply taking the elevator upstairs to his room.

Once the three were alone, Ahmed turned to Vladimir. "I feel too good to leave. Let's go to the bar."

"Definitely," Vladimir said and turned to her. "Come, Alexandra, join us for a drink now. Your duties as a translator are finished."

"I'm tired," she said, shaking her head. "I think I'll go home."

"I won't take no for an answer. You've been most helpful tonight and deserve a reward."

She studied the two men. Vladimir's eyes glinted — from the wine or the lighting, she wasn't certain. Ahmed had a similar glow about him. "I appreciate the offer, but I need some sleep."

"I've already given you the day off tomorrow. You can stay with us for a while. Please?"

He took her hand and swung her arm like a child. She glanced over her shoulder toward the exit and sighed. The streets weren't safe at this hour, and she couldn't afford an official taxi. Besides, she hadn't missed how Vladimir swayed as he tugged on her arm. If he were to drive in this condition and the police stopped him…She shuddered. She couldn't bear the thought of someone else falling into the same problems as Yuri.

"All right, I'll come with you, but you have to agree to let me drive you home."

Ahmed applauded. "Excellent. You add much to our celebration."

"Thank you," Vladimir said, kissing her lightly on the cheek.

The lobby bar was a dark wood and brass alcove set to one side on the first floor of the hotel. A small stage housed some instruments left by the loud rock band that had played earlier in the evening. The three took seats at a small table in a corner where they continued drinking and toasting their good fortune. Only when the bar closed did Vladimir bid a noisy farewell to all and permit her to lead him to his car.

Once at his building, she helped him to his apartment. At the door, he protested loudly when she tried to take her leave.

"Stay here with me tonight," he said.

"No."

"At least come in with me." He swayed slightly on his feet. "You don't want me to fall and hurt myself."

She glanced through the open doorway. She could see the kitchen door from there and shuddered involuntarily. She shook her head. "No, I can't."

"Come in," he said, pulling on her arm and taking a step inside.

His insistence was getting a little annoying. She jerked back on her arm, causing him to tumble to the hallway floor. He howled in pain.

"Get up," she said, tugging on his arm to drag him inside the apartment. He blinked at her, and giving her a slightly crooked grin, yelled louder.

Locks clicked on another door on the hallway landing. A bald-headed man stuck his head out of a crack in the doorway.

"What's going on out here?"

"He fell, that's all," she said over Vladimir's continued whimpering.

The neighbor squinted first at Vladimir, then at her. "Stop the racket, or I'll call the police. You can't disturb everyone in the middle of the night like this."

"I'll help him inside now," she said to the scowling neighbor, and pulled Vladimir to his feet.

Giving her a triumphant smile, he quieted down, and the neighbor harrumphed and shut his door with a solid bang.

She slung Vladimir's arm about her neck and half pulled him into the apartment, kicking the door closed behind her. Once inside, he straightened up slightly and walked on his own to the couch. Dropping onto its cushions, he patted the place next to him.

"Sit with me. I want to talk to you for a little bit. We never have time to talk at the office. There, it's all business."

"No. I'm tired. I want to go to bed."

He gave her another crooked smile. "You could sleep here."

She remembered that smile. The same one from the alleyway

on graduation night. This time, however, only one of them had been drinking. "No. I want to go home."

He stood, took a moment to steady himself, and stumbled to her, slipping off his coat on the way. She took a step backward. Her heel touched the door. No room to retreat. Reaching her, he put his hands on either side of her head, effectively trapping her between his arms. He leaned closer. She could smell the alcohol on his breath. Her own came in quick pants.

"Please," he whispered. "Stay."

His mouth closed over hers. Her ears rang. She could now taste the vodka on his lips, his tongue. Her knees trembled, and she wasn't sure she could remain standing. His arms slid down the door and enclosed her. She leaned into him to keep from falling, and he pressed himself against her, whispering her name into her ear.

Pulling back enough to gaze into her eyes, he brushed a stray hair from her face and smiled at her. "Do you know how long I've waited for this moment? Ever since that night. I've been patient, my dear. Do you have any idea how it hurts to watch your love marry another?"

She lowered her gaze and then raised it to meet his. "You could have had your pick of any woman. There had to have been others."

"Not any like you." He touched her chin with his finger. "Haven't you wondered why I never married? I've had my taste of other women, but once I got to know them, I found them lacking. None compared to you."

She gave him a halfhearted smile. "It's the drink talking. Let's get you to bed."

She slipped from between his arms and led him toward the bedroom. He followed obediently. At the bedroom entrance, he pressed himself against her back. Reaching over her shoulders, he unbuttoned her coat. It slipped from her shoulders and onto the floor. His hands fumbled with the zipper on the back of her dress. As if in a trance, she let her body respond to his attentions. The dress was off now, and she shivered in the bedroom's coolness. His hands touched her bare skin and tiny electrical shocks skimmed across her skin from the points of contact. When had Yuri last touched her with such tenderness?

Yuri.

She flinched and backed away from him.

"No," she said, stooping to pick up her clothes and spinning about to face him. "I-I can't. It's too soon."

He took a stumbling step forward. "How can you say it's too soon? I've waited practically my whole life."

She ducked around him, heading toward the front door. He grabbed her hand before she'd taken two steps. "You're not leaving, are you?"

"You're drunk. Go to bed."

"Please don't be mad at me." She felt him caress her wrist with his thumb. "Stay with me for a while. We can sit on the couch and talk about old times. I promise I'll be a gentleman."

"No. I've got to go."

She'd been closer to accepting his offer than she liked. As much as she hated the thought of going back to her dark apartment, she hated the thought of betraying Yuri's memory even more. She stumbled to the door, fearing he would follow her, try to stop her. Instead, he simply called her name.

After dressing in the hallway, she hurried down the stairs and let the cold air clear her head. With a glance over her shoulder to assure herself he hadn't followed her, she began the cold walk home. The subway and bus systems had long ago shut down for the night. She could hail a gypsy taxi, someone looking for a few extra rubles, but those driving about at this hour could be as drunk as Vladimir. She pulled her coat tight about her, deciding it best to risk going on foot.

No sooner had she found the sidewalk than a black Volga pulled to the curb in front of her. Her heart quickened and she glanced about, seeking a place to run. When the front passenger window lowered and a man called her name, she froze in her tracks.

"It's dangerous for such a young woman as beautiful as you to be alone at this hour," said the FSB agent. "Let me give you a ride home."

She searched up and down the street, desperate for some type of escape.

"I assure you, I'll be more of a gentleman than your friend." His knowing smirk was infuriating. "Allow me give you a ride. Besides, I have the information you asked for."

Considering her options a moment longer, she remained on

the sidewalk. He opened the car's rear door and beckoned to her. Desperate for both warmth and information, she acquiesced.

Sergei gave an amused chuckle and put the car in gear.

"I'm waiting," she said.

He checked her in the rearview mirror. "Things not go well with your boss tonight? What happened? Did he become too fresh?"

"None of your business. I agreed to come with you for only one reason, and I'm still waiting."

"Did he confess something tonight? His undying love and devotion?"

"You seem to know everything. You tell me."

"Love can make us do strange things, you know. It can make us betray another. Even the best of friends will go at each other's throats when love is involved. I know. I've seen it happen."

Her ears buzzed. The man kept talking, but the buzzing grew louder, and she could no longer hear his prattle. It didn't matter. She had gotten his hint immediately. Vladimir had done it. Vladimir had given Yuri's name to the police.

The ringing was so loud, she thought she would scream in pain. "Stop the car," she shouted, her hands over her ears.

Sergei turned the car back into the curb. She fumbled with the latch, but finally opened the door and stepped onto the curb. The full cold hit her in the face, and she fell to her knees. She bent lower and vomited into the snow on the other side of walk. Her sobs mixed with her gagging. Tears streamed down her face. When her heaving finally subsided, she gulped in the frigid air to clear her head.

A hand cupped the back of her neck, and another, her elbow. Sergei helped her to her feet, and when he spoke, his voice showed none of his earlier mocking. "Please, let me help you into the car so I can take you home."

❧

At her apartment building, she refused his offer to assist her inside.

"I know you've had a shock. We'll talk again, later," he said after scrutinizing her a moment longer.

As soon as she let herself into her apartment, she continued to the bathroom, pulled off her clothes, and stepped into the shower. Using the hottest water she could tolerate, she scrubbed herself until her skin stung to remove any traces of Vladimir's cologne or the lingering scent of vomit. When her skin glowed red, she turned off the hot water and gasped as ice-cold needles of water numbed her further.

Afterward, she shuffled to the living room and sat on the couch, pulling the phone toward her.

Lena answered on the second ring.

"Can you call me back?" Alexandra asked her before she could say more than "hello." "I can't afford an international call."

"No problem."

While she waited for Lena to return her call, she pulled a business card from her purse and stared at the tiny Cyrillic print. Deep in thought, she jumped when the phone rang.

"Is Nadezhda all right?" Lena asked.

"Fine. She's fine."

"Then you aren't. You wouldn't be up at — what time is it there? Three?"

"I just…I guess…" she said, forming the words around the lump in her throat. "I'm just lonely."

"Dear friend. Of course you are. I wish you could come here."

"I'm working on it, but it seems to be further away than ever. I can't believe I could be so wrong about so much."

"You've always been an optimist. You see what you want, especially in people."

"My blinders have been taken off tonight."

"What are you going to do about it?"

She stared at the card in her hand again. "I have an idea."

"I've got to go. Fred will be wondering about the phone bill. I'll check on you tomorrow."

"That won't be necessary. I'll be busy."

After she hung up the receiver, she let her hand rest on the hand set for a moment. Lifting it again, she dialed the number on the card.

"Nikolai Borisovich Kamovski?" she asked when a voice grumbled in response at the other end. "This is Pavlova, Alexandra. We need to meet to discuss my future employment…Two o'clock? I'll be there."

She replaced the receiver and stumbled to her bedroom. Curling into a ball, she pulled the covers tight and tried to sleep.

Chapter Twenty-Two

Sergei cursed himself the whole drive home. He may have pushed this rabbit too hard. Turning someone required delicacy. A person needed strong motivation to betray a friend or loved one. He thought he'd had the right approach when he showed her Vladimir was not all he appeared.

But he was lying to himself. Sharing Vladimir's involvement in Yuri's death went beyond trying to get her cooperation. The other man's relationship with Alexandra also bothered him. She deserved better. His hands still ached from gripping the steering wheel when he observed her tender care for Vladimir at his building. The intimate way he'd leaned on her shoulder. And she'd been in there much too long to have merely accompanied him to the door.

After parking his car in front of his own apartment building, he remained seated behind the wheel. The thought of returning alone to his dark apartment suffocated him. Even the car's confines seemed preferable to the apartment's echoing emptiness. The car's temperature dropped, and his breath formed small clouds in the halo from a nearby streetlamp.

The cold seeped through his coat, clearing his thoughts. He remained in the freezing car to punish himself for what he was contemplating. No way could he become emotionally involved with this rabbit. The first rule of turning: recognize them for what they were, a means to an end. Not the end itself.

His breath condensed on the windows and frosted the glass. The light from the street highlighted the crystal patterns forming on the windows like so many puzzle pieces. So pretty, so delicate. If he placed his palm on the window, the frost would melt and then refreeze into a different pattern. Not unlike how he'd desired to change Alexandra's view of Vladimir.

He banged on the steering wheel, the pain serving as an additional punishment. Despite wanting to drive her away from Vladimir, he hadn't meant to wound her so deeply. He probably had destroyed his best link to finding out Ahmed's purpose to coming to this Russian backwater.

With a sigh, he threw his shoulder against the car door to open it. He would have to figure out how to salvage the damage he had caused tonight. And it would be easier to do in a warm apartment.

Chapter Twenty-Three

Alexandra tugged at the short skirt, trying to make sure it didn't expose anything from behind. Tanya, a dark-haired Ukrainian, watched in amusement. She sat on a bench in the cramped dressing room in the back of the casino, a cigarette dangling precariously in her fingers.

"Don't worry," Tanya said, blowing cigarette smoke toward the ceiling. "You get used to it after a while."

"I hope so." Alexandra gave her a weak smile back. "How long have you been working here?"

"Long enough not to mind the skirt or the men who put their hands up it."

"What do you when they do that?"

"Smile at them and hope they'll stick some money in your panties next time."

Alexandra studied her reflection in the mirror on the wall of the small room, giving her skirt one last tug. When she had arrived at Nikolai's casino for work, a burly man named Misha had handed her the skirt, a low-cut white blouse, a pair of black stockings, and very high heels and pointed her to the room, grunting something about changing. Several other women, including Tanya, were already there preparing for the night shift.

"You really are new to this, aren't you?" Tanya chuckled. "What did you do? Follow some man out here on the promise of marriage?"

"I'm paying off my husband's debt to Nikolai."

Tanya snorted, blowing smoke out through her nose. "Let the deadbeat pay it himself."

"He can't. He's dead."

Tanya's mouth formed a small O, and she glanced away. "Sorry. This job has turned me into a cynic. My boyfriend paid for me to come here with a promise of marriage. When I got here, I found out he was already married. With a baby. He wanted me to be his mistress. I left him, but here I am in the middle of Siberia, and no way to get home."

Before Alexandra could ask her more about the place, the door opened, and Misha's bulk filled the hole. "We're opening soon; get to your places."

"Keep your pants on, Mishinka." Tanya stubbed out her cigarette and rose slowly. "It's not like this place is packed every night."

Misha grabbed her arm and glared at her. "Watch your mouth, bitch. Nothing would give me more pleasure than to teach you how to show respect."

"Bruises are bad for business, baby." She jerked her arm from his grasp and pushed past him into the hallway leading to the casino.

Alexandra followed her, but Misha put his arm on the door jam, blocking her way. She couldn't help but notice his forearm was the size of her waist. "The boss said some special people will be here tonight. He wants you to take care of them because they speak English."

"What do you mean, 'take care of'?"

"Wait on them," he said with a shrug. "Take their orders. Sit with them. Make conversation."

"Which ones are they?"

"You'll know when you see them."

He dropped his arm and let her pass. She stepped into the casino's main room. Nikolai had renovated some interior rooms in one of the old Soviet hotels. Located on the fourth floor, it had no windows, and the dim lighting gave it a sense of eternal midnight. Disco music blared from a stereo system in one corner next to a small dance floor where colored lights rotated about the empty stage. In another corner, a dour-faced man tended bar.

A group of small, round tables with chrome chairs separated the bar and dance floor from the gaming tables. A man in a tuxedo stood at attention behind the roulette table. Tanya leaned on the blackjack table, her chin in her hands.

After her eyes adjusted to the light, Alexandra scanned the room. They had already opened the casino, and two men sat feeding coins into the slot machines flanking one wall. On the other side of the room…she swallowed when she recognized the "foreigners."

Ahmed sat in deep conversation with other men. A young blond man also sat with them.

Misha gave her a shove from behind. "Go on, get over there and entertain them."

She stumbled slightly, recovered her footing, and advanced to the table. Giving a tentative smile, she said, "Hello, Ahmed."

"Alexandra? What are you doing here? You know, Vladimir is very worried. I cannot get him to even talk about our project with Mr. Dehghani, so I have been dealing with other work these past two days. All he has done is search for you. It was very bad of you to disappear like that. How did you get here?"

She shifted her weight unsteadily on the high heels. The shoes were already pinching her toes. Vladimir had called her yesterday morning. She had hung up and taken the phone off the hook. Something inside told her to let him believe his behavior had angered her. After that, she'd moved in with a friend on the excuse she had no hot water in her apartment and sent Nadezhda to stay with Yuri's parents.

"You know," Ahmed said, motioning her to take a seat at the table, "he doesn't remember much of that night. I'm afraid we both drank too much. He is sorry if he, how you say, offended you."

After catching a glimpse of Misha's glowering face, she slid into the seat, perching herself on the edge.

"We are here to celebrate." Ahmed continued. "I brought my colleague here to get to know this young gentleman better." He waved his hand at the blond man seated with them. "Let me introduce you."

"We know each other," she said. "How are you, Piotr? It's been some time since we've seen each other."

"Yes." The man gave her a nervous smile. "I was sorry to hear about Yuri."

"Things happen," she said flatly. "Can I get you something to drink? That's my job."

"As I said," Ahmed said, "we are celebrating. What about some champagne?"

"Russian or imported?"

"Imported, of course."

She started toward the bar. Misha, who had taken his place as head of security by the front door, walked over and stood in her path. "What are you doing?"

"They want some champagne. I was going to get it."

"Nikolai said you were to spend the evening with them." He signaled to the bartender. "Bring a bottle of the French champagne to that table." Turning back to her, he said, "Now get back over there."

Taking her seat again, she said, "The champagne will be here in a minute."

"Wonderful," Ahmed said. "Let me introduce you to Mr. Shirazi. He is a university professor. A biologist."

"How do you do?" She held out her hand.

Like Dehghani, he didn't take her hand, only bowed his head at her. He was clean-cut and wore a suit. His shirt was buttoned to the top, but he wore no tie. His dark, wavy hair was brushed back from his face, giving him a cultured look.

"Exactly what are you celebrating?" she asked.

"Our good fortune. Mr. Shirazi is here to recruit scientists for an exchange program. Piotr has been selected. He will be leaving for Iran shortly."

She forced a smile instead and turned to Piotr and spoke in Russian. "Congratulations. I had no idea you were interested in leaving the country."

"Thank you." Piotr shifted uneasily in his chair. "It's a great opportunity to continue my work. You should see the facilities. And the pay. Enough to take care of my whole family. So much better than the Americans."

"The Americans?"

"You must have left the Institute before they came. They also offered money to supplement our salaries to continue research. Of course, not as interesting as the projects we had before. This offer is much better."

"Really?"

"You know," Piotr said, turning to Mr. Shirazi and speaking in English, "Alexandra also worked at the Institute."

"Is that so?" Shirazi asked. "In what area?"

"Nothing exciting," she said. "Vaccines."

"She's being modest," Piotr said. "Not only was she in charge of her division, she was also an artist. Making vaccines cannot be done by cookbook. It takes skill and intuition. She has both. She would put a little bit of this, a little bit of that, and you would have your vaccine."

"Please, Piotr, it's in the past. I quit all that after Nadezhda was born."

"Her daughter has a heart problem," Ahmed said, shaking his head, "and now she is a widow."

The cell phone on Ahmed's hip rang. Flipping it open to see who was calling, he excused himself and walked toward the door, talking on the phone along the way.

The bartender arrived and passed out champagne glasses to all. After glancing at Ahmed and seeing him still conversing on the phone, Mr. Shirazi turned to her. "I'm sorry to hear about your daughter. You know, we have some very good doctors in Iran."

"We have some very good doctors here too," she said. "Unfortunately, they say she needs to see a specialist in the West."

Mr. Shirazi paused for a moment. "If you were to work in Iran like Piotr, we might be able to arrange a trip to the West, or bring a specialist to our country."

Her heart skipped a beat. Was he actually offering what she thought? "What kind of work?"

"Vaccines. Just like here. We have some very good equipment, the most modern available."

"You should see it," Piotr said. "I've seen pictures of the labs. Incredible. I've also spoken to other Russians already there. They're free to work and not worry at all about money."

She drew in a breath and considered the idea for a moment. To work in a lab again. Her heart quickened just thinking about returning to her passion. Piotr's description was true. Creating vaccines was an art, and she was good at it.

"I don't do that work anymore," she said after she let reality return. "It's too dangerous."

"She thinks it's the work that made her daughter's heart bad," Ahmed said, returning to his seat.

She stared at the man, unable to contain her surprise. How had he learned so much about her?

As if he read her mind, he shrugged and said, "Vladimir told me of your problems."

"Now, no more business talk," Piotr said, raising his glass. "We're here to celebrate my good fortune. A toast to our night together."

After clinking their glasses, Ahmed turned to her. "I want a dance."

He stood, grabbed Alexandra's hand, and pulled her to her feet. About to protest, she caught a glance of Misha's glare in the corner of her eye and obediently stepped onto the dance floor.

Ahmed moved to the disco beat blaring from the speakers, and she followed his lead. They hadn't been dancing long when some sort of confrontation occurred at the door. Misha was arguing with a man trying to enter. The man pushed past him and marched toward the two of them with Misha close behind.

"So you took Nikolai up on his offer," Vladimir shouted over the music as he neared them. "What's the matter — wasn't my help good enough for you?"

The two stopped dancing, and she understood who had called Ahmed earlier.

The foreigner stepped forward, placing himself between her and Vladimir. "My good friend. I'm so glad you could join us. See? I told you she was here. I have been watching over her. Now you've found her, and we can get back to work."

Misha stepped up behind Vladimir with a snarl. Vladimir ignored him and glared at Ahmed. "Step aside. This is between me and Alexandra."

"This isn't the time for a discussion," she said, stepping from behind Ahmed. "I'm working. Go. Now."

"No. I want to stay and talk to you. You don't answer the phone. You never come to your door. Your in-laws won't tell me where you are. I was planning to wait outside their door for you. I knew you would at least see Nadezhda. All I want to do is to apologize."

"You've done that. Now go."

"But you haven't accepted. You haven't forgiven me."

Misha placed a giant paw on Vladimir's arm. "You heard her. She said go."

Vladimir pulled against Misha's grasp, but the man held tight and pulled him toward the door. Vladimir's face reddened as he struggled to keep from being pushed out of the casino. He shouted over his shoulder. "You'd rather dance and wait on strange men than to be with me? Fine. Good riddance, whore."

Misha's reaction was swift. His punch jerked Vladimir's head back and sent blood spurting from his nose.

"This is a legitimate establishment," he said. "We don't like people insulting our customers or our employees. Get out and stay out."

After shoving him out the door, he signaled to two security guards to escort Vladimir outside. With Vladimir disposed of, he marched back to the dance floor. "You've certainly made a great impression the first day on the job. You have any more boyfriends who're going to disrupt this evening?"

"I am not pleased either," Ahmed said, glancing about nervously. "We only wanted a quiet evening out. I think we should leave."

He walked back to his table and spoke to the others. They stood, and Ahmed dropped some bills onto the table.

Alexandra glanced around her. All other activity had stopped during Vladimir's outburst. Some customers were still observing her and the foreigners. One man in particular seemed very interested in the action on the dance floor. Their eyes met for a moment before he turned back to the slot machine. She stared at his back. Something in his clothes, his manner, reminded her of Sergei.

Ahmed's table was now empty except for the glasses and ruble notes. With a shrug, she returned to the bar for a tray and cleared the table.

While thankful for Ahmed's departure, she worried over her confrontation with Vladimir and the brief meeting with Piotr and the Iranian recruiter. Had she lost an opportunity to help Nadezhda? The offer to move overseas had been attractive enough for Piotr. Her skills were better than his, better than almost all her colleagues. Until the meeting with Piotr, she'd forgotten how much she enjoyed working at the lab.

After returning the dirty items to the bar, she followed Misha's hand signals to take the other patrons' drink orders. She visited the roulette table first, but the two men were too busy placing their chips on the various numbers. They waved her away without moving their gaze from the spinning wheel. Continuing to the slot machines, she approached the first man, who also waved her away. The second placed an order between shoving the coins into the slot. When she returned with his drink, he placed it by his smoldering cigarette and paid her without slowing his rhythm.

The only other customer was the one who reminded her of Sergei. He sat in front of one machine, playing with the coins more than slipping them into the slot.

"May I take your order?" she asked.

"Gin and tonic."

When she returned with his drink, he held out a bill, then pulled it back before she could take it. "You certainly know how to cause a scene."

"It wasn't my doing. I was just there."

"Your friend seemed rather upset with you."

"He's not my friend."

"Maybe you could use some friends," he said, running his hand up her arm.

"I don't think so."

His grip tightened on her arm. "Well, Sergei thinks so."

"Tell Sergei he should be out catching real criminals instead of harassing innocent people."

"Are you innocent?"

"Of course," she said tugging her arm out of her grasp. "Aren't you afraid of being identified as FSB?"

He picked up the glass, held it to his lips, and studied her over the rim. "We only make ourselves known when it doesn't matter."

"You want me to know I'm being watched. Enjoy. I'm afraid I have a very tedious life."

"That incident earlier wasn't boring."

"It was also unusual. I need to take an order from that table over there," she said, spinning on her heel.

Her hands shook, making the tray rattle. She'd done nothing wrong, but guilt was often immaterial in these matters. The KGB by any name was still the KGB. Still feeling his gaze on her back, she glanced in his direction. He absent-mindedly fed a coin into the machine while keeping his gaze on her. A shiver ran down her spine, and she retreated across the room to the blackjack table.

When she reached the table, someone called her name from across the room. She flinched, fearing the FSB agent had decided to ask her more questions. Instead, Ahmed waved at her when she turned around. Never had she thought seeing Ahmed would bring her relief, but she smiled at him when he approached her.

"We never finished our dance," he said.

"I, uh, I'm working," she said, glancing toward the door to check on Misha's whereabouts.

"No problem. I talk to him. I'm special customer."

He sauntered over to the door and spoke briefly with the man.

Misha frowned, glanced at her, and curtly nodded his head. He signaled to another girl at the bar to take her tray.

"See," said Ahmed when he returned. "Everything is fine. You dance with me and the other girl carries drinks."

"All right," she said, handing over the tray.

Once on the dance floor, he drew her close and swayed to the music. He whispered in her ear, "My friends wanted me to deliver a message to you. They would like to meet with you."

Her heart pounded. She hadn't lost the opportunity. Not completely. But how did Ahmed play a role in this? "What exactly is your relationship to Mr. Shirazi?"

"Mr. Shirazi and Mr. Dehghani — they are my clients. I help them find the things they are looking for. Vladimir has some things Dehghani would like. You are something Shirazi wants. I bring together, and they pay me to do so."

"I'm just another commodity to you, then?"

"No. You are more than that." He pulled back slightly and brushed the hair away from her face. "You are beautiful woman. You deserve better life than this. I can make it better."

"In Iran?"

"You talk to Shirazi. You work in Iran, he will help you find a doctor for Nadezhda. We will meet after work. Two friends having breakfast. No one will notice."

"So you know the FSB's watching?" she said, glancing over at the man at the slot machines.

"He, or one of his kind, has been my companion since before Mr. Dehghani arrived." He laughed. "I think they want us to know we are being watched. No problem. We have ways to avoid them, if we want. It is a game. You will meet me for breakfast?"

"I guess it would be all right to hear what Mr. Shirazi has to say."

Ahmed spun her around and pulled her close again. "We'll

meet after work. I promise it will be interesting."

He swayed with her through one more song. When the next tune began, he escorted her off the dance floor. At the bar, he raised her hand and pressed his lips against it. Bowing slightly to Misha at the door, he strode out of the casino. Out of the corner of her eye, she saw the FSB agent follow and allowed herself to relax.

Once alone, she realized Ahmed had placed a card in her hand. Turning her back to Misha, she glanced at the piece of paper. Shirazi's business card listed his title as a cultural officer for the Iranian government with phone numbers in Tehran and at the Iranian embassy in Moscow. She slipped the card into her skirt's waistband and returned to the blackjack table to retrieve her drink tray from the other waitress.

"Don't accept less than two hundred," Tanya said.

"For what?"

The Ukrainian rolled her eyes at the other waitress. "It. He's a foreigner — and rich. All foreigners are. Tell him you want two hundred."

She felt the blood rise in her cheeks. "I'm not…He's not…"

Before she could explain more, she caught Misha's stare. He waved her toward a table of new arrivals, and she left without completing her thought. Continuing to make the rounds, she decided it best to let the others think what they would about her. The true story was complicated, and even she was not certain exactly where the full truth lay.

Chapter Twenty-Four

Sergei squinted at his alarm clock. Three o'clock in the morning.

Who could be calling at this hour? With great effort, he pulled himself out of bed and shuffled across the bedroom and tiny hallway to the phone. It continued to shrill on the table in the living room, and he stubbed his toe on the sofa leg as he reached for the receiver.

He was still cursing when he spoke into the mouthpiece. "Borisov, damn it, here."

"Sir?"

Pavel. What did he want at this hour? He was supposed to be watching the girl.

He shook his head to remove sleep's cobwebs and ignored the dull ache in his foot. "Sorry. I hit my foot. What's happened?"

"It's the girl. I followed her to a casino. She's working there. Serving drinks. She met some people there. Ahmed and that Iranian from the embassy."

"The one talking to the scientists?"

"Yes. Then Morozov appeared and created a disturbance. They all left, but Ahmed returned. I think he delivered a message from the Iranian."

"Why's that?"

"He danced with her for a little bit, and then left. No gambling; no drinking."

Sergei rubbed his toe. He needed a cigarette. He glanced about the room, spotting a pack on the table, just out of his reach.

"Just a minute."

He lit a cigarette and inhaled the smoke, letting its taste fill his mouth and throat. The rush of nicotine further cleared his head. He knew what the Iranians were offering. Unfortunately, it was not illegal to go to work outside the country. If she had still been employed at Viru-Preparat and privy to current state secrets, they might have been able to deny her an international passport, but she had left too long ago to make that argument.

"Sir?" his telephone called faintly.

He picked up the receiver. "Sorry again."

After another draw on the cigarette, he blew out the smoke and watched the cloud ascend to hover slightly below the ceiling. "Pavel, does your family still have that dacha?"

"Yes, sir, we do." Pavel's voice sounded suspicious.

"No one's there right now?"

"No, sir."

"Can I borrow it?"

"Now, sir? In the middle of winter?"

"It does have a fireplace?"

"Yes, but I'm not even sure you can get there — "

"Good. Come by. Drop off the keys and directions. I'm going to borrow it for a morning. After that, you can go to bed."

"All right, sir." The phone clicked in his ear.

With a chuckle, he considered his subordinate's reaction. Most Russians had a dacha, a country home. "Home" was, however, an exaggeration. For some Russians, it was no more than a hut or glorified storage shed. Others, however, were two- or three-room wooden houses on a small plot of land.

Regardless, Russians cared about the land, not the house. Those small plots had sustained the average citizen through seventy years of Soviet rule and ten years of democracy. In the spring, they planted beets, potatoes, tomatoes, cucumbers, and squash; in the fall they canned the harvest; and in the winter, they lived off what they had grown. For all their sophistication, most Russians had not totally denied their peasant roots, and it had served them well.

Such a spot was the perfect place to have a private conversation with Alexandra. He could discuss the situation with her in a more formal setting, complete with all the fear it created, but he knew she'd shut down and not hear his warning. He was beginning to admire her fight, and he wanted her to win it, but honorably.

He inhaled heavily on his cigarette, making it burn quickly toward the end. After extinguishing what was left in the ashtray, he limped back to his bedroom to dress. A long night awaited him if he would have the dacha ready for his meeting in the morning.

Chapter Twenty-Five

Alexandra took her time changing after the casino closed. The other women had teased her throughout the rest of the shift about her upcoming date with Ahmed.

"You're sure you want to meet this man?" asked Tanya, pulling a sweater over her head. "I can't stand foreign men. Too hairy. Like apes. Russian men have such smooth chests like babies."

"I wouldn't know."

"You will soon enough. The only way you're going to be able to pay off that debt is by making extra money on the side."

Alexandra said nothing but busied herself with her stockings, her cheeks now burning hot.

Misha opened the door.

"Don't you ever knock?" asked one of the other women. She jerked her shirt closed. "We're changing in here."

"That's what he's hoping," said Tanya. She stuck a cigarette in her mouth and lit it. "It's the only way he ever gets to see any skin."

Alexandra suppressed a smile, but the others laughed out loud. Misha's face hardened. "You girls wish you could have a chance at a real man like me instead of those losers you usually drag home."

"They aren't losers. They can afford me," Tanya said. She

blew smoke toward the ceiling and slung her coat over her shoulder.

He gave her one last stare before turning to Alexandra. "You tell your boyfriend not to come here again. We don't want anyone making trouble for our customers."

"He's not my boyfriend. I have no control over him."

"If he shows up, Nikolai said I was to make sure it's his last time."

"I don't care what you do to him."

His gaze scanned the room. "You have one minute to get out or spend the night here."

Turning on his heel, he marched out and shut the door with a bang. Tanya puffed on her cigarette again. "I bet he's covered in hair."

"Like a Siberian bear," another said, making all of them laugh.

They gathered their things and some paired off to continue arm in arm through the casino.

Outside, their laughter echoed off the buildings lining the street. The area was deserted except for them. Light from the streetlamps gave their shadows long legs stretching across the wide sidewalks and onto the buildings.

Alexandra spotted Ahmed's black Mercedes up the street just at the edge of a streetlamp's halo. She waved goodbye to the others and picked her way through the icy patches on the sidewalk toward the car.

The passenger door opened when she approached, but before she could get inside, someone grabbed her arm and pulled her away from the car. She didn't recognize Vladimir for a moment. Bandages covered his nose, and bruises circled both eyes.

Recovering from the shock of his appearance, she jerked her arm from his grasp and backed away. "Leave me alone. I don't want to see you."

"You have to talk to me. Let me apologize. I know I've acted like a fool, but it's because I love you."

"But I *don't* love you. Don't want to talk to you. Don't want to see you. Leave."

He stepped toward her, and she backed away. Ahmed appeared between them once again. She hadn't even seen him get out of his car.

"Come, old friend, let her go," he said, placing a hand on his arm. "I promise I will care for her."

"Why can you trust him and not me?" Vladimir's forehead wrinkled, and for a moment, she thought she saw tears glisten in his eyes. "He doesn't care about you. I'm the only one who has your interests at heart. I deserve at least an opportunity to talk to you."

She remembered his compassion and care after Yuri's death, and her resolve softened for just a moment. Then she remembered who had been behind his death, and her hands clenched into fists.

"What I do or where I go is my decision. You don't control me."

Vladimir opened his mouth to say more, but stopped. A shadow passed behind her, and Misha stepped into the streetlamp's light. He was wearing a heavy fur coat, and she recalled Tanya's remark about the Siberian bear. His dark eyes twitched, and she almost expected him to growl. Instead, he grasped Vladimir by the arm, wrested him from Ahmed's grip, lifted him off his feet, and snarled into the bandages. "Haven't learned your lesson? I told you to stop bothering my girls."

"She's your girl, now?" He twisted in Misha's grip to glare at her. "Just how many men do you have?"

Misha gave him a shake. "Show some respect."

"I just want to talk to her. Alexandra, please, let's go somewhere where we can be alone."

"It doesn't appear she wants to go with you." Misha twisted Vladimir's arm behind him and turned him away from her.

Vladimir howled in protest. Struggling in Misha's grasp, he shattered the early morning quiet, shouting insults at the top of his voice. A *militzia* officer stationed further up the street turned in their direction and marched toward them, his black-and-white striped stick swinging freely on the strap around his wrist.

As the policeman approached, Ahmed whispered to her, "Let us go. Leave him to Misha."

Ahmed had retreated and just opened the car door when the officer joined them. "What's happening here?"

She checked behind her. Ahmed signaled her to join him, but the officer stopped her.

"Where do you think you're going?"

She turned to the policeman and heard Ahmed start the car behind her. Her stomach tightened at the thought of losing the same opportunity a second time.

"I-I was leaving."

The policeman gazed behind her. "That may be difficult."

She heard the engine rev and the tires crunch on the snow before she could even turn around. The officer motioned her to step with him toward Vladimir, still squirming in Misha's grasp.

"This man was bothering an employee," Misha said. "He made a scene last night, and now wants to continue."

"I just wanted to talk to her," Vladimir said. "She's a friend."

The officer studied her, Misha, Vladimir, and the neon casino sign at one side of the hotel's entrance. His gaze finally rested on her. He pointed at Vladimir with his stick. "You know him?"

She nodded.

He turned his attention to Misha, his eyes hard. "Let the man go."

Misha dropped Vladimir's arm.

"Even if she is an 'employee,' this is between them. Get going."

Misha raised his hands in a gesture of surrender and stomped away.

After watching Misha's back for a moment, the officer said, "From now on, keep your arguments indoors. If I come over here again, I'll arrest both of you." With that order, he spun on his heel and marched back to his post.

Once alone, Vladimir said, "That's a good idea. Like I said, let's go somewhere to talk."

Alexandra crossed her arms. "There's nothing to talk about."

He grasped her elbow. His tone was soft, but his grip firm. "I think I deserve an explanation for your change. If it's about the other night…"

Even through her coat, she could feel his strength, and for the first time, she feared what he might do if they were alone. "Please, not now. I'm tired."

He pulled her gently, but determinedly, toward his car. "I promise to take you home afterward. There's so much you don't know. So many things I need to tell you. You're in danger."

Her boots slid on the icy walk. She could not break away from him without making a scene and calling the policeman to them again. The officer's reaction the first time didn't suggest he would be much help.

When they reached Vladimir's car, someone grabbed her other arm and pulled her in the opposite direction. "Hey, where do you think you're going with my date?" a man asked.

Both she and Vladimir turned toward the voice, and Sergei grinned at them.

To her surprise, Vladimir's grip loosened, and she fell into Sergei's arms. He immediately wrapped his arm around her waist.

"Who are you?" Vladimir asked.

"I could ask the same of you," Sergei said. "I made a date last night with this woman. For breakfast."

"Another one? I thought you were leaving with Ahmed."

Her thoughts spun wildly. Why hadn't she been quicker about getting in the car with the man? Now she had to choose between the FSB and Vladimir.

"No. I mean, yes. You see, we were — we were going to talk for a minute."

"You'll talk to this stranger before you'll talk to me?" Vladimir squinted at her. "Fine. But I still want my explanation."

He stamped to his car and spun his wheels on the ice as he drove away from them. After he turned the corner, she turned to the agent. "You can let go of me now."

"I'm not so sure," he said, the corners of his eyes crinkling around them. "I kind of like it."

"Well, I don't," she said, stepping away.

"Stop," he said. "You're coming with me."

"No. I have things to do."

"You mean finding Ahmed?"

"How did you — "

She stopped herself. The man at the casino last night must have told him. Her heart squeezed. "Are you arresting me?"

"No, but I did promise you breakfast."

He replaced his arm about her waist and firmly directed her toward a weathered Zhuguli parked several cars behind where they stood.

"What happened to the big Volga you had the other day?" she asked.

"That was an official car. This is my own. This is not official business, so no official car."

"Just because I work in a casino — "

"I assure you, my intentions are honorable. Are yours?"

"What does that mean?"

"Let's discuss this over some nice, fresh eggs, shall we? I know a wonderful little place out of town much more intimate than my office."

Before she even knew she'd agreed, she was seated next to the FSB agent as he drove away from the casino and toward the city's center. They continued through the tall apartment buildings of a sleeping district. When she realized they were leaving town and asked where they were going, he refused to say more than "for breakfast."

The buildings gave way to the countryside. The sky now glowed pink, coloring the snow-covered fields behind barbed-wire fences. Wooden houses set back from the road peeked from behind bare birch trunks. In the end, she crossed her arms and stared straight ahead. Out of the corner of her eye, however, she could tell he kept glancing at her.

A while later, he turned off the paved road onto one of frozen mud and skillfully avoided the gullies threatening to swallow the car. At the end of the lane, he pulled to a stop in front of a green wooden house with gingerbread trim. She studied him with narrowed eyes. "This is no restaurant."

"I never said I was taking you to a restaurant. I said I'm taking you for breakfast."

After helping her out of the car, he held open the creaky gate surrounding the dacha's small front yard to let her pass. Once inside the fence, he raced ahead of her on the snowy path to the front door and unlocked it for her.

Inside, a dying fire gave the front room some warmth, but not enough to eliminate a damp, musty smell. She could tell no one had occupied the house for several months. Taking off her coat, she hung it on the hook by the door and placed her boots on a mat next to it. As soon as he removed his coat and boots, he went to the fire and tossed some more logs on the embers. Shortly, the wood blazed a bright blue.

He rubbed his hands together over the hearth and smiled. "I came here earlier to set things up for us so we could have some time to talk. Now, I'll make you the breakfast I promised."

He left her to warm her hands by the fire. In the next room, she could hear a clattering of pans and feeling curious, joined him in the kitchen. Leaning against the doorjamb, she studied the room.

A gas stove and rusted sink took up the space along the back wall's windows. Poles and stalks poked through the snow in the backyard, marking a garden plot covering most of the area within the fence.

He turned and shot her a quick smile. "Which would you prefer? Eggs? Bread and meat? Cheese? Yogurt?"

She shrugged. "Whichever."

"Eggs, then."

He lit a burner on the gas stove and set a skillet over it. Taking several eggs from a bowl by the sink, he soon had them sizzling in the skillet. The aroma coming from the stove made her stomach rumble.

Unable to contain her interest any longer, she asked, "Why did you bring me here?"

"I've never been one to leave a damsel in distress," he said, stirring the eggs. "You seemed to be in need of rescue back there."

"It's obvious you planned all this. Why?"

The spatula suspended in midair, he stopped playing with the eggs in the skillet. "I wanted to talk with you off the record. Share some things with you. Things you need to know."

"And they are…?"

"In a moment, but first, breakfast."

After sliding the eggs onto two plates, he placed them on the table, already set with silverware and steaming cups of tea. With a deep bow, he said, "Madam?"

After a moment's hesitation, she took the seat he offered.

He pushed the chair in. "Bread?"

"Please."

He put a loaf along with a knife and butter in the center of the table and took the seat opposite her. "Eat."

She took a bite. "Not bad."

"It's very difficult to ruin eggs, although I've known people who could," he said, smiling at her over his fork.

"Where's your family?"

"Family?" he asked, a confused expression on his face. "Oh. You mean the pictures in the other room. This isn't my dacha. I'm merely borrowing it from a friend. That's his family. I'm not married. I was, but not anymore."

She placed her fork on her plate and glared at him. "We're having breakfast. I'm tired, and I want some answers. Why bring me here?"

He leaned back in his seat. The amusement she had sensed in him disappeared. "Because I need you. Just like you, I have a lot of questions, but you're the one with the answers."

"I told you before, I'm not a traitor."

"Even after what you found out about Vladimir? Betraying a traitor — "

"That's between us. I can handle him."

"Yes, my dear, you were doing very well when I arrived." The amusement reappeared for a moment. "But I see you getting into even deeper waters. The Iranians — "

"Are offering jobs. Can you say the same thing? All I have left is Nadezhda — "

"That's not all you have left. You still have your dignity and your life. As you keep telling me, you've done nothing wrong — yet. But if you continue — "

"Are you threatening me?"

"No, warning you. Until now, you've been involved with only minor players, Vladimir, Nikolai, even Ahmed. But when you start talking to the Iranians, things become more serious."

She stood, barely keeping her voice in an even tone. "I thank you for the warning, but understand this — I'm going to do what's best for me and my daughter. They're offering me more than you can."

"So, you're available to the highest bidder?"

"If it will help my daughter, yes."

"Then why don't you go back to Vladimir? He could provide for Nadezhda."

The question stopped her next remark in her throat. She slumped back down in her chair, her hands falling limply onto the table.

"I knew you had more pride than that," he said, his voice softening. He reached across the table and touched her hand. "I've seen your fire. I just don't want it to burn you."

She glared up at him, snatching her hand away. "Take me back. I let you make me breakfast and listened to what you had to say. I've kept my part of the bargain."

He leaned back, studying her. He opened and shut his mouth as if he thought better of his response. Finally, he said, "All right. But I promise you, our next meeting will be more official."

Chapter Twenty-Six

Sergei stomped his boots on the mat inside the dacha's door to knock off the snow. His steps echoed in the empty house. After leaving Alexandra at her apartment, he'd returned to clean and lock up Pavel's summer home. The fire had died, and he shivered slightly when he hung his coat on the hook by the wall. He stepped to the fireplace where a few embers still glowed.

After scraping the ashes and coals into a small bucket, he tossed the whole mess into a snow bank beside the back door. The sun, so bright earlier, now hid behind a layer of gray clouds. The snow hissed, steam rising from holes the coals melted into the ice and blending into the dull sky.

In the kitchen, he washed and dried the plates and utensils, putting them back where they belonged. Living alone certainly had forced him into new avenues. He'd become a true domestic, having developed his housekeeping skills — such as they were — after his divorce.

He frowned. Alexandra had been forced on a different path as well. What if Yuri hadn't died? How long would their marriage have survived? What role would Vladimir have played in her life then?

And without her involvement with Vladimir, Pavel would never have brought her to Sergei's attention, or to the disaster of a breakfast.

Instead of gaining an informant, he'd pushed her straight

toward the Iranians. A part of him could see the appeal. The Iranians offered her what her own country couldn't. Under the Soviet system, life had been predictable. Then the whole system had turned on its head with the criminals more in control than the ones who were to enforce the law.

All the same, he admired her tenacity. She was going to do what she thought best for her child.

With everything back in its place, he walked back through the house to the front door. He caught sight of the family photos Alexandra had seen earlier. Pavel, his wife, his parents, and a small child smiled at him. Now their smiles seemed to mock him. He'd been so confident when he brought her here, so certain he'd be able to make her see his side.

Of course, he still held one card. One piece of information that might convince her to see his point of view, and more importantly, put what she thought she wanted in a new light.

Chapter Twenty-Seven

I want to thank you for meeting me at such short notice," Alexandra said, offering her hand to Mr. Shirazi.

"Not at all." As before, he did not take her hand, but indicated a seat at the table across from him. "The company of a beautiful lady is always welcomed. What can I offer you? Tea? Coffee? Juice?"

"Tea would be nice."

"Very well," he said, waving to a young man standing in the doorway.

While they waited for the man to return, Mr. Shirazi asked, "Did you have any trouble finding the building? It is rather out of the way, but much more discreet."

The young man placed a cup and saucer in front of her and poured tea into the cup from a small white pot.

"You gave excellent directions to the building. Of course, it did take me a while to find your offices inside."

"The building housed a factory that was abandoned two years ago. We were able to rent these offices very cheap." He leaned back in his chair and studied her. "So, you have come to discuss our offer further?"

Alexandra cleared her throat. "Ahmed passed your message. He made it sound rather appealing. I've had a chance to rethink what you said and what he said, and I would like to know more about this exchange program."

"It is very simple." He poured tea into another cup for himself. "You come to Iran, work with our scientists. We pay for your travel, provide you housing, pay you a decent salary…" He raised his hands, palms up. "A very convenient arrangement for both you and us."

"What exactly would I be working on with your scientists?"

He leveled his gaze at her. "As you know, Iran has many enemies. Beyond the Great Satan of the US, some of our other neighbors also pose a risk. We must be prepared to defend ourselves against all aggressors, all who would oppose us. Some of these countries have powerful weapons more deadly and insidious than a thousand nuclear bombs. We all know there are other types of arms out there as well."

"Biological weapons." She nodded. "I'm certainly familiar with them."

"Your friend Piotr highly recommended your talents," he said, giving her a slight smile before taking on a serious tone. "Do you know how many missiles are pointed at our capital? You would be working to help us defend ourselves against such warfare. Our enemies all say they are not working on such things, but we know better, don't we? Just as Russia must be prepared, so must Iran. We are asking you to continue the work you used to do and are quite willing to pay appropriately for it."

"I don't know," she said, shaking her head. "There are risks involved in such work."

"Thinking of your daughter, are you not? I assure you we will be able to get her the finest care available."

"There is a doctor. I have his name. An American who has a new technique just for her problem."

"An American would be difficult. You know we do not have good relations with the US. Other places and other doctors, however, can be considered."

"Ahmed said something about helping me get to the US."

"Did he? Perhaps he has some other prospects I am not aware of." He leaned forward, resting his arms on the desktop. "Of course, we have no direct ties with the US, but there are ways to arrange immigration in the future after you have completed your contract with us. Or perhaps another country?"

"How would I be accepted as a woman?"

"As a scientist and a foreigner, you would live and work in a special compound. Your daughter would attend a Russian-speaking school. It would almost be as if you were still in Russia."

"You make it sound rather appealing. What kind of vaccine work would I be doing?"

"We know countries are making some deadly combinations. Imagine anthrax mixed with something else. You would be working on vaccines against such diseases."

"Developing a vaccine means having the original virus to work with. You have such combinations? Where do you get them?"

"That is something you needn't worry about," he said, waving his hand as if chasing away a fly. "My question to you is if you would be interested in doing such work. Surely you cannot be happy waiting on men who grope you? Or even as a secretary who types letters and answers the phone? I am offering you a chance to do what you were trained to do and to make a better life for you and your daughter."

"Of course I don't like waiting tables. But I also don't like being in debt."

"We can take care of that. Your work to us is more valuable than what your husband owes at the casino."

Her gaze shot to the man's face. How did he know? Ahmed, of course. She shifted in her chair and decided to change the subject. "There's the matter of my in-laws. I don't want to leave them behind."

"They can come, too, if they wish. You would need help to care for your daughter, after all."

"This is all very generous, but I'll have to think about it."

"I can assure you the work you do for us would be most appreciated, and we will show our gratitude appropriately. You will find our laboratories and equipment are the most modern money can buy. Besides Piotr, several more of your colleagues have already left for Iran. I would be glad to let you talk to them if you wish."

"You make a persuasive case." She checked her watch. "I'm afraid I have to get to work shortly."

"Of course. Please, feel free to call me at any time. I will be here a few more days."

"Thank you," she said, standing.

"I'm sure we can work out an arrangement most satisfying to

both of us," he said, rising with her and flashing a smile.

He escorted her through the empty factory to a metal door at the side of the building, their footsteps echoing among the rusted machinery. After a deep bow to her, he opened the door, and she stepped outside.

In the waning afternoon light, she got her bearings and picked her way through the factory yard to a gate in the wooden fence surrounding the building. As she passed onto the street, a man stepped in behind her and grabbed her elbow.

"Alexandra Alexandrieva," Sergei said in an authoritative voice, "if you will follow me."

Tightening his grip on her elbow, he propelled her down the street toward a black Volga waiting by the sidewalk.

"I told you the next time would be official," he said through thin-pressed lips.

At the car, he opened the door, helped her in, got in beside her, and nodded to the driver. The car pulled away from the curb and entered traffic leading into town. The back of the driver's head looked vaguely familiar.

She glared at Sergei. "Where are we going? I have to get to work."

"You just met with Mr. Shirazi, didn't you?"

"I don't have to answer that."

"It doesn't matter. We know you did. Care to tell me the subject of your discussion?"

She stared straight ahead, saying nothing.

"I know that too," he said, crossing his arms across his chest. "You discussed his 'scientific exchange' program. About how you might work on vaccines in Iran. What did he offer you? Money? Trips to Europe? Maybe medical care for your daughter?"

She whipped her head in his direction, certain he could see her heart pounding against her ribs. Had the FSB bugged Shirazi's office?

"Yes, that's it." A smirk flitted across his lips. "Help with your daughter's heart problem. Did he tell you what the cost would be for your daughter's health?" The man leaned back against the car's seat. "Tell me, Alexandra Alexandrieva, what do you know of your father's death?"

She willed her face to remain passive, to give no indication of the panic welling within her. Were there no secrets this man didn't know?

"That he died in a laboratory accident?" he asked. "An explosion? That the body was burned, and there was nothing to bury? The body was burned, but not in a laboratory fire. They incinerated it to prevent what he carried from spreading."

He pulled a brown envelope from his overcoat, opened it, and removed some photographs. When he tossed the first one onto her lap, she gave it a cursory glance, then picked it up to examine the image more closely. She recognized her father's face immediately. A typical head shot for the Institute's files.

A second photo fell onto her lap. The same man, only slightly older with graying hair, a slightly thinner face, and sunken eyes — almost malnourished in appearance.

"This photo was taken two days after he was exposed to a virus he had been mutating. A careless mistake. Failure to adequately restrain a laboratory rat. It moved, and his assistant stabbed him with the needle. He had been working on a new form of Ebola. The doctors could do nothing for him but keep him sedated and watch the course of the disease."

He tossed the rest of the photos one by one onto her lap. Each successive photo showed progressive deterioration of the man's face. In each, her father appeared more gaunt and skeletal. Blood appeared around his eyes in one. Rivulets were shown streaming from his nose and mouth in the next. The final photo showed a living corpse with eyes staring emotionlessly ahead.

Covering her face with her hands, she spoke through her fingers. "Put them away, please."

She could hear him shuffling the photos as he spoke. "Did you know samples of his blood were saved and used to create an even purer form of the virus? He died as a hero of the Motherland. Of course, they could never acknowledge it outside of the laboratory."

When she lowered her hands, the photos were gone. Her hands dropped to her lap, and she twisted her fingers together as he continued in a slight monotone. "What the Iranians want you to do is protect their own people while they perfect the manufacture of a virus that could kill all their enemies."

"You've got it wrong," she said whipping her gaze to him. "They want to protect themselves from those who already have it. According to you, the virus already exists, and we are the ones who have it. Why shouldn't I protect others from what killed my father?"

"Where do you think the Iranians get the viruses they want you to work on? From scientists who care more about themselves than what happens to the rest of the world and are willing to sell state secrets to the highest bidder. And once the Iranians have the vaccine, what would stop them from using the virus? Against Israel? The Americans? Us?"

Alexandra studied the back of the driver's head. She recognized him now. He'd been at the casino, playing the slot machines.

"As you said, you've done nothing wrong," Sergei said. "I can't hold you on anything. Only appeal to your sense of patriotism and humanity."

The driver pulled the car to the curb, parking in front of Nikolai's casino. Sergei got out and helped her out of the car. On the sidewalk, he held her hand for a moment. The touch was soft, intimate, as was a brief instant when their gazes met. "Ask yourself if you wish your father's fate on anyone else."

"I have to go to work now," she said and withdrew her hand from his.

She turned on her heel and moved as if in a trance toward the hotel's entrance, not noticing the casino's flashing neon sign, nor those passing her on the street.

The blank stare accompanying her father's last breaths of life remained seared on her retinas, overshadowing all else.

❧

Alexandra dropped her keys and coat on the floor as soon as she entered her apartment. Vladimir hadn't made another appearance, and Ivan had replaced the locks for her, so she felt secure in her apartment for the moment. Her mother-in-law's scolding about the slovenly way she shed her clothes on her way to the bathroom rang in her head, but she merely shook it off. At least she wasn't there to do it in person. She glanced at the clock in the hall. Four o'clock in the morning. She would catch a few hours' sleep before visiting her daughter, only to return to the casino and start the routine again.

Sitting on the edge of the tub, she pulled off her boots and rubbed her aching feet. Between the long hours waiting tables and the high heels they required her to wear at the casino, the muscles from her toes to her waist screamed in protest with every movement. After starting the water to fill the tub, she trudged through the apartment's small rooms, dropping the rest of her clothes as she went. After a few minutes, she found herself in Nadezhda's bedroom. The soft, sweet smell of her daughter made tears prick her eyelids. Retrieving a blanket from the girl's bed, she held it and breathed in her scent.

With a shake of her head, she tried again to block out the memory of her father's face in the photographs Sergei had shown her. Still carrying the blanket, she slowly toured the room, her fingers brushing against different objects. At the dresser, she paused, and her hand rested on the little ice-fishing bear she had bought in Moscow when Lena married.

She lifted the toy and moved it slowly to make the weight rotate and the bear's arm jerk up and down. Despite her weariness, she smiled as she remembered the happiness she felt for her friend that day. The toy dropped back to the dresser top when the memory continued to Vladimir's fateful phone call.

She returned to the bathroom, removing the last of her garments as she went and eased herself into the warm water. As she soaked her sore muscles, different images drifted through her mind. Nadezhda in the hospital; Yuri's legs swinging in Vladimir's kitchen; Mr. Shirazi's smiling face; Vladimir's drunken grin; Sergei's mocking smirk. Finally, her mind returned to the photos of her father.

When the water cooled, she pulled herself out of the tub and shivered as the air hit her. She welcomed the shock as a way to clear her head. Wrapping herself in a heavy robe, she stepped over the trail of clothes and retrieved her purse.

After a brief search, she found the card at the bottom of the bag and studied the writing before shuffling to the phone.

Someone answered before the second ring.

"Hello," she said. "I need to see you…Yes, I know where it is…About four will be fine…I'll see you then."

After she hung up, she staggered to the bedroom and stretched out on the bed, hoping she'd made the right decision.

Chapter Twenty-Eight

Sergei replaced the receiver and smiled. He'd done it. He'd turned her. True, she hadn't said she would help him, but the call meant she'd selected her path. Had the photos been the key? He'd taken a risk showing them to her. They could have easily turned her against the Motherland.

The phone rang again. Second thoughts already?

"*Aloa*," he said into the receiver.

Pavel's voice scratched over the connection. "Sorry to wake you."

"No. It's all right." He rubbed his hand over his face. At least it wasn't the rabbit. "What's happened?"

"It's Morozov."

Did he detect something in his voice? A hesitancy? He sat up straight on the sofa. "What it is?"

"He's disappeared."

"What?" he asked, standing up, as if he were going to run out into the street and catch the man.

"I've been at both his apartment and his office." Pavel's voice was actually trembling. "I'm sorry, sir."

Sergei took a deep breath. All that work. He paced in the space between the couch and the table, dragging the phone cord behind him like a thin tail. "Don't panic. We need to find out if he's left the area. I'll take the train station. You check the airport. They'll have a record if he's been through either one. After that, we'll check the jail and the hospitals."

"Yes, sir." Pavel sounded more secure.

"Call me after you've contacted the airport."

After Pavel rang off, Sergei dialed a number at the agency headquarters.

"Alexei," Sergei said when the person answered, "call your contact at the train station. Find out if a Morozov, Vladimir Stefonovich has purchased a ticket for tonight…No, I don't know where…No, I don't know when…If he has, but the train hasn't left yet, let me know immediately…Better yet, let me know immediately either way, if he's on a list or not."

Sergei slammed the receiver into its cradle. So close. Had his advantage just run out? With the girl on his side, he only needed time before he found out what Morozov was up to.

A moment later, he dialed Marcus's number. He didn't miss the irony that outside of Pavel, the person he trusted most was an American CIA agent.

Chapter Twenty-Nine

Alexandra stepped off the bus, headed up the street, and then turned, managing to get back on the bus just before the driver closed its doors. Several stops later, she got off that bus and took an electric train in the opposite direction. She had no idea if this would actually fool anyone, but felt she had to at least try to make it difficult to follow her.

The bus carried her out of town. At the third stop, she descended and spotted Sergei's car parked nearby. After she sat down, he pointed the car back into town.

When he parked in front of an ordinary apartment building, her forehead wrinkled. "I thought you said our next meeting would be official. Why are we here?"

He gave her an annoying but now-familiar smirk. "My apartment. I'm still not ready to make things 'official.'"

"You're trying to keep me a secret? Why? Are there spies among the spies?"

"It's probably best not to be quite so curious."

He got out, but she remained seated, studying the drab concrete exterior.

"You wanted to talk. Are we going in or not?" he asked as he leaned into her door.

The conviction she'd felt when she made the call was now fading with the afternoon light. Only the recollection of her father's photo forced her to let him help her out of the car.

As before, Sergei had prepared the place for her. Open-faced cheese and salami sandwiches and a jar filled with flowers sat on a table in his living room located to the right. In the kitchen, an electric samovar popped and hissed as it kept water hot for making tea. To her left, a shut door. She assumed it led to the bedroom. She jerked her gaze from that direction.

After offering her a seat on the couch, Sergei poured each of them a cup of tea and settled into an overstuffed chair next her. "What changed your mind?"

She watched the steam rise from her cup and blew on it, sending a series of ripples across its surface.

"Nadezhda," she said after a moment more of thought. "Actually, one of her toys. For the longest time, I've felt pulled in all directions. Yuri, Vladimir, Nikolai, Ahmed, you. I decided I was going to take control of my future. I know what I want. I want to help my daughter. Whether I can fix her heart or not, I can't let someone release something into the world that could kill her or others."

"I'm glad I was able to convince you to see it my way."

"Before we go on, there's one thing I must know," she said and sought out his gaze. "Why should I trust you?"

"Because like you, I'm interested only in saving people. That's been my problem. I've always been interested in the real criminal. The one who destroys our country out of corruption or greed. The politics of it all holds no interest to me. That's what has kept me here in Siberia instead of moving up and into Moscow."

"I'm simply supposed to believe you are doing this for pure altruism?"

A bemused smile crossed his face. "I guess so."

"It's not easy to trust the KGB. No matter what you call yourself, you're still KGB."

"It's not easy trusting citizens anymore, either."

"So our collaboration is based on mutual distrust?"

"If it need be so," he said, leaning forward. "Now, tell me what you know."

"You agree our relationship is based on distrust, and then you ask me to tell you what I know?" She laughed. "You are an enigma."

"All right. Then I'll begin. Your friend Vladimir is in the hospital. He had us worried for a while. We couldn't find him. He checked himself in after the scene he made on the street. He says it's because of his nose, but it's clear he's hiding."

"He wouldn't be the first Russian businessman to hide in a hospital. There's no better security. But from whom?"

"I'm not sure. It could be Nikolai. After causing a scene two days in a row at his casino, the man couldn't be happy, but hardly angry enough to make Vladimir fear for his life. No, I think it's someone else he fears."

"The Iranians."

It was a statement, not a question.

"He's been dealing with them," he said with a grave nod. "We also know what they want. They want seed virus."

The blood drained from her head. "Vladimir? Seed virus?" She shook her head. It made no sense, and at the same time it did. "He never worked in that part of the Institute. He did know people in that area — "

"Like your friend Piotr."

The statement put her on alert. How much did the man actually know? She searched for the right phrases. "Piotr did have something to do with viruses, but he never really — "

"I have his files…all of them. I know exactly what he did. You don't have to cover for him."

"It's not that." She stopped and took a sip of tea. "There are — were — a great deal of security measures and precautions to keep anyone from removing a virus. You can't simply put it in your pocket and carry it out. Most of the time, the virus is not that stable. Exposure to sunlight, for example, destroys most."

"Most, but not all. We need to know what virus Vladimir's trying to, or has already been able, to obtain. And how he got it. This is where I need your help." He reached across and took her hand. The familiarity of the gesture was almost too much for her. She tried to wrench her hand away, but he held firm. "What I need you to do is contact Vladimir. Apologize to him. Make up with him. Get close to him again. He would most certainly tell you something to give us some answers."

She stood and tugged harder on her hand. His grip tightened. Unable to release herself from his grasp, she turned her back to him. She stared out the window. Despite the somewhat early hour, the sky was growing dark. Streetlights glowed against a blackening backdrop. Above them, thick clouds threatened to drop their snow at any moment.

"Get close to Yuri's murderer? I-I can't. You're asking too

much."

He stood now, and drew her to him. With her back still to him, he spoke softly into her ear, his breath upon her cheek as he whispered. "I told you it wouldn't be easy, but you're used to sacrifice. Think of what you've done to get your daughter what she needs. You say you want to give her a future. Have you forgotten your father's pictures so quickly? Imagine it being your precious Nadezhda instead. And not one child, but thousands, millions. All writhing in agony, blood running from every orifice, unable to even cry…"

"Stop it!" she cried, shoving herself away.

This time, he let her go. She put her hands over her ears, but turned to face him. "I always knew the FSB were experts in torture, but I never knew you could be so cruel."

"Perhaps you're right." He raised his hands and dropped them. "Perhaps you're not the person for such a job. Other avenues exist, but they might not accomplish what I desire — to stop this madness completely. Cutting out Vladimir would end this one exchange, but unless we're able to expose the whole operation, another salesman would appear."

After she mulled over his words, she raised her gaze to him. "I can't go back to Vladimir, but there may be another way. You said he's in the hospital. No one will be at his office. I still have a key. We could go search for the answers there."

"You think we haven't looked? Our resources may not be as deep as they once were, but we still know how to search an office and a home."

"But you don't know exactly what to seek. I have a better idea of what might be of interest to you."

"Very well. Let's see if you're more clever than my agents. Come on."

He took her hand again. This time, she didn't resist.

"Where are we going?" she asked, letting him lead her toward the front door.

"Vladimir's office, of course."

Chapter Thirty

*O*nce in his car, Sergei allowed himself to glance at Alexandra, recalling the touch of her hair on his cheek when he had spoken into her ear. Each time the streetlamps illuminated her profile, he felt his pulse quicken slightly. He had to remind himself he had considered her suspect. He admired her persistence, her conviction, her *gumption*, as Marcus would say. This tenacity raised her above those who merely accepted the changes after the fall of the Soviet system as part of being Russian, but kept her from joining those who used the situation to their own advantage.

He drove past Vladimir's office building without slowing.

"What're you doing?" she asked. "The office is back there."

"The back entrance will be less conspicuous."

After turning into an archway in the building about halfway down the block, he parked in the courtyard behind a building next to Vladimir's office. Darkness provided them additional cover, particularly with so few streetlamps in the courtyard actually working.

Taking her hand, he helped her out of the car. "If anyone sees us, we're just two lovers taking a stroll."

She nodded and allowed him to lead her toward the building. Approaching the entrance, she heard a noise to their side that made him tug her close. Before she could protest, he placed his lips against hers. He enveloped her in his arms, and his heart quickened as her breath accelerated. He pressed her against him, taking in her scent, the softness of her mouth upon his.

Behind them, a set of footsteps faded away.

She stiffened and thrust him back. "They're gone now."

In the semidarkness, he watched her trembling hand touch

her lips. When was the last time his kiss had affected a woman? More importantly, when had a kiss affected him so?

His pulse still raced, and he could feel the blood rushing to his groin. After several deep breaths of cold air, he managed to push down the feelings surging through him. By the time Alexandra had stepped to the office's back entrance, he was once again in control of his body and emotions.

Without another word, she heaved the wooden door open. Their footsteps echoed in the concrete hallway. At the office door, they paused again. He listened. Hearing nothing, he gave her a nod to open it.

Once inside, she reached for a switch, but he stopped her. "The light can be seen through the window. There may be others interested in what's going on here." He pulled a flashlight from his jacket pocket. "Use this."

She moved to Vladimir's office and cracked the door. "It doesn't look like anyone's been here. Are you sure your agents searched here?"

"You only know we searched if we want you to. An overturned plant. Some misplaced papers. Consider it a calling card, if you wish."

He stepped past her into the office and closed the blinds before flashing the light about the room. He waved the light toward the computer. "Can you turn that on?"

"Yes, but what are we looking for?"

"You tell me. You said you thought you might find something my agents missed."

She flipped the switch. The machine hummed to life, its screen casting a bluish glow. "I don't know if you'll find anything in his computer. It was more for show. I did most of the typing on the other one."

"Then we should start with the papers," he said, flipping off the machine. Opening one drawer after another, he glanced at the contents of each until he found one with files. He removed the first file and handed it to her. "Start here."

She shuffled through the papers inside and sighed. "These are letters I typed." Taking the flashlight from Sergei, she shone its beam across the folders in the drawer. "More letters I typed."

She passed the light over the desk and studied the papers scattered across the top; she turned the pages in his appointment book, spun his Rolodex file, and riffled through a stack of notes on one corner of the desk.

While he pretended to skim the contents of one folder, he observed her examination of the desktop out of the corner of his eye. In a move so subtle he almost missed it, he caught her palm one slip and place it in her pocket. The rabbit still had some fight left. Let her think she had succeeded in fooling him. He'd learn what she'd found soon enough.

After a few more minutes of file skimming, he straightened and stretched his back. "I don't see anything I haven't seen before. You finished?"

She nodded but didn't raise her gaze to meet his. "Not a very wise idea after all. It's growing late. I need to get to the casino."

"You're still going to work?"

"Is the FSB going to pay my debt?"

"We don't pay even for dinner, regardless of how pleasant the company."

"Then I'm going to the casino. Any chance the FSB will at least provide some transportation there?"

"It could be arranged."

He could also have Pavel enjoy another night of gambling. The man had better keep a closer eye on her than he had on Vladimir.

Chapter Thirty-One

Alexandra straightened her spine before knocking on her in-laws' apartment door. Her whole body ached from eight hours on her feet, even after the bath, but she had something to do before she could take a nap. Throughout her shift at the casino, her mind kept wandering back to the piece of paper resting in her coat pocket. She was certain Sergei hadn't seen her put it there, but the other FSB agent's presence all night at the slot machine suggested otherwise. Let him follow her. Nothing out of the ordinary for her to go to her in-laws'. They were keeping her daughter, after all.

Quick footsteps answered her knock, and the door swung open to reveal Nadezhda, her blue eyes wide with surprise. "Mommy, Mommy." She glanced past Alexandra. "But where is *Dyedushka*? He went to the store for *Babushka* and has been gone ever so long."

"I'm sure he'll be back shortly," she said, her exhaustion disappearing in her daughter's presence. She stooped down and scooped up her daughter, giving her a tight hug.

Nadezhda put her thin arms around her neck and squeezed back.

"Did you come to take me home?"

The question brought a lump to Alexandra's throat. "No, my dear, I can't take you home just yet."

"Why can't I be with you?"

The question seemed so simple, and the answer so

complicated. She searched for an answer that would satisfy her daughter.

"Because I'm working at night, and I have to sleep during the day." She put the child down and pulled off her coat. Hanging it up on a hook by the door, she caressed her daughter's head. "I want to be with you too. I promise I'll work things out."

A heavy footfall signaled her mother-in-law's appearance. Katerina's stout frame and short, tight blond curls made her resemble any number of retired Russian women.

"I don't see how that girl has any heart problem," Katerina said between gasps. "All that energy of hers keeps mine pumping too fast. When she heard the knock at the door, she ran away from me so fast, I couldn't catch her."

"I know she can be a handful. I don't know how I would have managed without you, though. Thank you."

"It's the least we can do after the mess Yuri left you in," Katerina said, kissing her on both cheeks, and then the first one again.

"The milk has been spilled," Alexandra said.

Katerina searched her daughter-in-law's face. "You look tired. I hope you're not working too much. Why don't you come into the kitchen and have some tea."

"That sounds good." She picked up her daughter's hand and spoke to Nadezhda. "Do you want some juice with me?"

"All right," the little girl said with a nod, "but *Babushka* says it can't be too cold."

Alexandra rested her hand briefly on Nadezhda's forehead. "Why? Have you been sick?" She glanced at Katerina for additional information.

"She's fine today," the older woman said, "but last night, she had a cough. The juice is a precaution. We don't want another bout of pneumonia."

Nadezhda scrunched up her face. "I don't like being in the hospital. The food's not as good as *Babushka* makes."

The two women laughed. Alexandra picked up Nadezhda and followed her mother-in-law into the kitchen. A kettle and pot of *kashi*, boiled buckwheat, simmered on the stove, giving the room a warm, moist feel. The butter plate sat on the counter next to the stove, and the table held three settings of orange-dotted plates and cups.

"We're just waiting for Ivan to return with some bread before we eat. He shouldn't be much longer."

"Nadezhda told me he went out."

Katerina set out another plate and cup, and Alexandra took a seat at the table. Nadezhda chattered to her mother about what she had been doing with her grandparents, stopping only when the front door opened. Ivan carried a net bag with an oval loaf of black bread. He handed the bag to Katerina and greeted Alexandra with the traditional three kisses.

"What a pleasant surprise. I thought you'd be sleeping right now."

"I just wanted to visit with you first."

"You need to eat more," Katerina said, slicing the loaf and spreading it with butter. "You're looking thin and pale."

Katerina served each of them bread, a bowl of *kashi*, and tea, then sat down as well. The adults ate and drank in silence. Nadezhda filled it with a detailed discussion of a neighbor's new puppy.

After a while, Katerina asked Nadezhda, "Have you finished?"

The child nodded.

"Good, let's go wash up, and then you can play in our bedroom. Let's go, my darling."

Nadezhda obediently slid off her chair. Before following her grandmother from the room, she hugged and kissed her mother.

"Will you be here all day?" she asked, drawing back in her mother's arms. "Not today, my sweet." Tears formed in Alexandra's eyes. "Like I promised *Dyedushka*, I need to go to sleep too."

"Why don't you take a nap with me later?"

"I'd like that very much," she said, squeezing her daughter tightly. "But there are some things I have to do. Another day, I promise."

"Good. Will you come tomorrow?"

"I don't know. I'll try. Now, go and play like the good little girl you are." With a final kiss for her mother, the child left the room.

"You should be spending more time with Nadezhda," Ivan said. "She asks about you constantly."

"I hope to put an end to this soon. I've found out some

things. Things that might help me out of this situation. But I still have some missing pieces. I'm hoping you'll know some of them."

Ivan got up from the table and poured himself another cup of tea. "Now I understand why you've come in the morning instead of the afternoon. What can I possibly do to help you? I'm an old man who lives on a pension that never comes."

She waited for him to seat himself again, placed her hand over his, and gazed into his eyes. "Ivan, I know about my father. I know how he died. He was infected with a virus he was working on at the Institute."

He jerked his hand from hers and rubbed a shaking hand over his face.

"H-How could you? That was a state secret. No one knew, but…" His face blanched. "The KGB. The KGB told you, didn't they? They were the ones who…Why? How? To what purpose?"

"To convince me to help them," she said. "I need to know more about the work he — you — did."

He stood and paced the floor. Running his hands through his thick, white hair, he spun about to face her. "Is that what you meant when you said you might be able to work things out? You've sold yourself to the FSB?"

"How dare you accuse me of such a thing," she said, rising to her feet. "Do you know how hard I'm working? All that Yuri has put me through?"

She sat back down at the table, covering her face with her hands. This was not going at all as she had expected. "I'm protecting you, in case you care."

She heard him sit heavily in his chair. When she peered through her hands at him, she noted his face remained drained of color. She pulled the piece of paper from her pocket and placed in front of him. "I took this off Vladimir's desk. I thought I'd managed to keep it from the FSB, but I'm not so sure now."

She told him everything, from Vladimir's call to her in Moscow to searching his office last night. Katerina stepped into the kitchen at one point, only to be waved out with a stern glance from Ivan. After forty years of marriage to someone who'd worked on state secrets, her mother-in-law had learned how to accept such a dismissal and retreated without a word.

"When I saw the paper, I recognized the handwriting immediately," she said. "I also recognized the name. I need to know why Vladimir wanted his name and number."

He stared at the piece of paper for a moment, then turned his gaze out the window. His voice had a faraway tone to it. "Vladimir came to me a few months ago. He said there was this exchange program for scientists, and he would pay me a finder's fee for those he could recruit. He was particularly interested in those working on viruses. I told him most of the people I knew had long retired, but Andrei was still working. I gave him the name and number."

He turned his gaze back to her. "He never gave me a ruble for the information, so I figured he'd never contacted him."

"Perhaps he didn't," she said with a sigh. "What was he working on at the Institute?"

"He was an administrator. You name it, he oversaw its production. Anthrax, Ebola, smallpox, influenza — and combinations of them."

"Combinations? You mean like what killed my father?"

"What killed your father was a crude mixture of Ebola and smallpox. With the advent of more advanced genetic techniques, we were able to create some truly virulent hybrids. And aerosol."

"But Ebola isn't — "

"Not normally," he said.

His voice lost its earlier emotion, and he continued in the detached fashion of a scientist. "But we created a mutation. With the addition of smallpox RNA, it was even more lethal than before. The mortality rate among the monkeys was close to one hundred percent. Of course, that was when we infected them at night."

"At night?"

"The virus was very unstable. It broke down quickly in sunlight. Even faster in aerosol form. But I doubt seriously Andrei was able to get any of these viruses out. You know about our security measures. You think we weren't concerned about what might happen if some of it was accidentally released? After what happened in Yekaterinburg with the anthrax incident? Seventy people dead." Ivan lowered his head. When he raised it, his voice was softer, pleading. "You have to understand. We considered ourselves at war. We were certain the Chinese were working on such things, as well as the Americans. We had to be prepared."

"But what about the treaties? The bans on such things?" she asked. "Surely you knew what you were doing was against international agreements?"

"Do you think we believed the Americans stopped because of such treaties? Regardless of what they signed or said publicly, we were certain they were continuing to work on them in secret, just as we were. My father was a soldier in the war against Fascism. I'll never forget the stories he told me about the hunger, cold, and death all around him. He helped liberate Leningrad after the siege. Do you know what nine hundred days of a blockade does to a city? How many people it kills slowly and painfully? I vowed I would help our country be strong and never let that happen again."

"Instead of killing slowly through starvation, you would kill quickly through disease."

He slammed his hand on the table, making the cups and plates jump. "Don't judge me. I did what I believed was right. I have no regrets."

"I'm not judging. I can't. I worked at the same Institute. I just never realized…" She raised her hands in a signal of defeat. "I guess I never truly understood the impact of what I — we — were doing until I saw those photos of my father. I can't let that happen to someone else. And I'm afraid it might."

"Andrei? You think he might have — "

"It's possible. That's why I needed to know what Vladimir might have gotten from him."

He ran his hand over his face and rubbed his chin. She could hear the faint scratching from his fingers passing over the stubble. "Of course, I've not worked for a while, but my guess would be the one that killed your father."

"That Black Pox?"

"Its research was the most advanced. As I said, we'd even tested it on monkeys. Since it could be transmitted through the air, secondary infections were possible, making it almost one hundred percent effective."

"You're talking almost complete infection and annihilation."

His gaze met hers. "That's assuming no vaccine."

The realization of all they had discussed hit her as hard as a blow to the stomach. She slumped in her chair. "That," she said, "would be my role."

Chapter Thirty-Two

*P*avel eased the large, black Volga through the traffic to the curb, slowing the speed to keep pace with Alexandra. A crowd had formed at the bus stop on the corner, but the stretch of sidewalk she traversed was almost deserted. Most of the shops located on the first floor of the surrounding buildings had closed for lunch, their interiors dark behind streaked windows in dull aluminum frames.

Sergei stepped out of the car and followed beside her. She glanced at him, and he gave her a knowing grin. Her head down, she increased her pace.

"Did you have a pleasant visit with your father-in-law?" he asked in a low voice.

She stopped and faced him. "I went to visit my daughter."

Her response told him everything, making him grin even wider. His intuition sometimes amazed even him.

After a moment, she continued toward the corner, him still at her side. "In my line of work, I've learned patience can be a virtue. If you don't want to tell me now, you can tell me later."

"There are some things I have to think through," she said without looking at him. "I'll call you."

He placed a hand on her arm. "I also came to warn you. Vladimir has checked out of the hospital."

"Why should it concern me?"

"You made me understand you didn't wish to see him. Aren't

you worried he might show up again at the casino?"

"If he does, I'll let Misha deal with him."

"Are you sure you don't want to share what you learned with me?"

She stopped again. Her gaze shifted back and forth between the bus stop and Sergei.

"I'm tired." She sighed. "I need to go home and get some sleep."

He gestured to the car now parked about half a block behind them. "I'll be glad to give you a ride."

"Your favors come with strings. I prefer the bus."

"Very well. You know how to reach me," he said and watched her move away.

After a moment, he nodded to Pavel. Before the man could steer the car away from the curb, an incoming bus angled in front of him and blocked the car's path. The bus's passengers drained out the exit at the back and headed toward Sergei. As he and the crowd met at the front of the bus, a heavy man appeared at his side. Sergei glanced at him. He wore a dark fur hat and a gray wool scarf wrapped over his face, covering all but his eyes.

The crowd thinned, and the man grabbed both of Sergei's forearms. Before Sergei could react, he felt his feet slide on the icy walk as the man propelled him toward the street and the front of the bus. Sergei struggled to reach his weapon, but his arms were pinned to his sides. With his assailant having the advantage, Sergei resisted as the man forced him to the curb where he gave him one final, hard push.

As he fell forward, Sergei realized the bus had folded its doors and belched a plume of burned diesel, signaling its departure. Sergei's last thought before his forehead hit the pavement was whether Alexandra was the next target.

Chapter Thirty-Three

When Sergei had turned back to the car, Alexandra had quickened her pace toward the bus stop. As much as she wanted to tell Sergei about the name on the piece of paper, she wanted to keep Ivan from being identified as the one who'd given it to Vladimir. Unlike in Stalin's times, those who reported on their family and neighbors were no longer considered heroes of the Motherland. By the time she reached the end of the queue at her bus stop, she decided now was as good a time as any to tell Sergei about Andrei and the Black Pox. If he asked about the paper, she would merely say she wanted to confirm her hunch.

With a sigh, she turned and pushed her way back to Sergei's Volga. She caught sight of him in the crowd at the front of the bus. A man wrapped in a wool scarf held him as if Sergei were a drunk needing assistance. At the curb, right in front of the bus, the man shoved Sergei with his shoulder, and the FSB agent toppled headfirst into the street.

Alexandra screamed. The man in the wool scarf jerked his head in her direction, and his gaze landed on her for a second before he ran away from the street and the crowd.

Sergei did not reappear, and the cloud of smoke from the bus meant it was leaving. Without thinking, she forced herself through those on the sidewalk, waving her arms at the bus driver and shouting that someone had fallen in front of his vehicle.

By the time she reached the bus and the curb, everyone at the bus stop was staring at her, and others closest to the bus had taken up her shouting. No one, however, had moved to help Sergei. He still lay facedown on the pavement. She knelt by his side. Someone else also stooped down. She glanced up, recognizing Sergei's driver.

Sergei's hand twitched. Together, she and Sergei's man rolled him onto his back. A scrape marked his forehead, blood trickling from the abrasion. His eyelids fluttered. She smiled at him when they opened a second later. The man put his hands under Sergei's shoulders, and between the two of them, they got him to his feet and onto the sidewalk.

The bus driver babbled at them from the opened door. "I didn't see. Thank goodness you did. I didn't understand what you were yelling about at first, but then everyone on the bus told me not to go."

"You should get him to a doctor," an old woman in the crowd said with authority. "That's a bad cut on his head."

Sergei reached up and touched the spot on his forehead. He stared at the tips of his gloved fingers as if trying to determine what had stained them. The dazed expression remained even when they helped him into the back seat of the Volga. Alexandra slid in next to him.

"Where should I take you?" Sergei's driver asked after positioning himself behind the wheel.

Sergei hesitated, as if translating the question. After a moment, he said, "My apartment."

Alexandra opened her mouth to protest but realized she was trembling from the sudden drop in adrenaline. With a weak nod, she rested her head on the back of the seat. Sergei did the same. By the time the car arrived, her head had slipped to rest on his shoulder.

At the apartment building, she and the other man helped Sergei up the stairs. Once inside, the two men conversed at the door in voices too low for her to hear. After the brief exchange, the other man nodded and left.

"May I take your coat?" Sergei asked when they were alone.

She started, as if waking from a trance. "I should be offering to help you."

"Nonsense, I'm fine. Thanks to you." He swayed on his feet. "Perhaps I should lie down."

"Here, let me help you."

He waved her away when she stepped toward him. After

pulling off his coat and dropping it on the floor in front of the rack, he lurched toward the living room. She followed him and sat down on the table in front of him as he stretched out on the couch.

"Your color is good, and your pupils are even. Do you have anything to disinfect the cut?"

"There's some iodine in the cabinet in the bathroom," he said. Before she moved, he added, "And a bottle of vodka in the freezer."

She smiled and nodded.

Returning with both as well as a clean cloth and a glass, she set them all on the table beside her.

Eying the single glass, he asked, "You aren't going to join me?"

"No. I'm sleepy enough without it."

After dabbing a bit of iodine onto a wad of cotton, she touched it to the wound on his forehead. He drew in his breath sharply. "Stop. I need the vodka first."

"Such a baby," she said, clucking her tongue. "You're worse than Nadezhda."

Leaning closer, she blew gently on the cut. Her face over his, he shifted his head to position his lips directly under hers, and she could sense their warmth. She stopped and straightened her back.

When she tried to rise, he grabbed her arm and tugged her back onto the table.

"Are you going to tell me now what you found out from your father-in-law?"

She sighed and stared out the window. The sun was still high enough in the sky to flood the apartment with a cold, bright light. "I found a piece of paper on Vladimir's desk. It held a name I recognized. Kirov, Andrei Fedorovich. He was an administrator at the Institute and oversaw a lot of the Institute's operations."

"Kirov, Andrei Fedorovich." He frowned, then winced. "I'll see what we know about him. You were in there a long time to gather just that bit of information. Something you already knew. Anything you'd like to add?"

She shook her head, unable to see how she could share more without mentioning Ivan's role. A yawn followed.

"Tired?"

Standing, she said, "I need to get home."

He raised himself to a sitting position and seized her arm.

"Stay. You can sleep here. What if I have some delayed reaction to the fall? I shouldn't be left alone."

"I think you'll be fine."

"No, I need you to stay. I want you to stay. It's safer."

"Than what? From whom?"

"Several possibilities. My investigation has obviously disturbed someone who believes they have enough immunity to attack an FSB agent. Think they'd hesitate to do the same to you?"

"All the more reason for me to leave. What if they saw me help you? Saw me come back to your apartment?"

Standing, he placed his hands on her forearms. "Please stay. I promise to be a gentleman. You can have my bedroom. I'll make some calls from here to find out more about this Kirov."

She returned his gaze. The argument made some sense. With no sleep for more than twenty-four hours, she was fatigued by the mere idea of traveling back to her apartment.

"All right," she said with a sigh. "I'll stay, but just for a short nap. Then I have to leave. I still have to work tonight."

He gave her arms a quick squeeze. "Follow me."

His bedroom was surprisingly neat, if not abundantly furnished. A narrow single bed and nightstand occupied one corner. A wardrobe stood in the opposite corner.

She lay down gratefully on top of the covers, and he pulled a blanket over her.

"I'll wake you in plenty of time for your job."

She smiled back and let herself drift to sleep.

❧

The sound and smell of frying *kalbasa* woke her. She tiptoed to the kitchen. Leaning against the doorframe, she watched Sergei expertly stir the sausages and onions in a skillet.

"Why is it you're always feeding me?"

"I think I enjoy mothering you a little." He pointed to the next room with the spoon he had been using to stir the skillet's contents. "You know where I eat. Please take a seat. I'll be in momentarily."

Shooting him a smile, she continued to the living room where he had already set two places at the coffee table. She sat down on the couch and told her stomach to quit rumbling.

He placed a steaming plate in front of her. "How did you sleep?"

"Not very well. What you said to me about them coming after me has me worried. What about Nadezhda? Sometimes family members…"

"I don't know." He frowned. "I'm afraid I don't have very good news about your friend Kirov."

Her fork stopped halfway to her mouth. "He's not my friend."

"Regardless, he's dead. A car accident two days ago."

"An accident. That doesn't mean — "

"It appears about as subtle as my fall in front of the bus. His car was definitely pushed off the road." He shook his head. "I'm sorry things have escalated as they have."

The full import of his words hit her straight in the stomach. "What am I supposed to do now?"

"Leave here. It's getting too dangerous for you."

She moved to the window and stared out. The sun had set and streetlamps made yellow circles of light below. She put her hand against the cold glass. "What about Vladimir? The virus?" Her breath fogged the window, obscuring the view.

Turning back to him, she wrapped her arms about herself, a cold dread enveloping her.

He stepped to her and folded his arms about hers. "I care more about you at the moment. I'll find out what I need from other sources. Perhaps it's time to bring in others. Poor Pavel hasn't had a day off since I began this investigation. If I told my superiors, I could arrange protection for you and your family."

"And where would I go? There's still Yuri's debt."

"What do you care about his debts to that scum Nikolai? Leave it and him behind."

She shook her head. How could she explain to him the obligation she felt to Yuri when she could barely justify it to herself? He'd killed himself from shame, and she couldn't let his death be tainted further. "No, you made me see there's more at stake here than just Nadezhda's survival. I have to help you see it to the finish."

With his hand under her chin, he tipped her head up and gazed intently into her eyes. He brushed a strand of hair from her face. "I could have you arrested."

"For what?"

"The interest of state security, if nothing else."

"You'd do that? Put me in prison?"

"Only to protect you."

He leaned closer, and his breath warmed her face. "I care for you, Alexandra. In case you haven't noticed. More than I should."

His lips touched hers, and she relaxed in his embrace. How long had it been since she'd felt safe in a man's arms? Clasping her hands behind his neck, she pressed her body closer to his.

He caressed her back, and a spark ran up her spine. She shuddered and let her own hands slide to his waist.

His lips moved from her mouth to her cheek, to her hair, to her neck. "Sasha," he whispered harshly into her ear.

The diminutive of her name was the equivalent of the Arctic air blowing outside. Yuri had used that name for her, in better times. She drew back and away from him. "I'm sorry, Sergei. So sorry. I–I…can't."

Without a backward glance, she rushed toward the front door, Sergei on her heels. "Alexandra, what is it? What did I do?"

"Nothing," she said, reaching for her coat. "Nothing. It's me."

He raised his arms in a gesture of resignation. "If you're not ready, I'll leave you alone. But don't go."

"I can't stay, either."

"Please. I promise to stay away from you, if that's what you want. Stay here where I know you're safe. If they came after me, they may come after you as well."

"And staying here is safer for me? *They* may have seen me leave with you. *They* may know we're together."

"When you're with me, I can protect you. If you leave, I…"

He stepped within inches of her. She could feel his heat, but when he reached across her, she recoiled. After taking the coat from her, he hung it back on the hook by the door. "Please stay. At least help me clean up after our meal."

She spoke to the floor. "I guess I can do that."

After they carried the plates and cups to the kitchen, she washed, and he dried and put them away.

The tiny kitchen made it difficult for them to avoid contact. His fingers grazed hers as he took each plate from her, and each time, her pulse would quicken, and the thrill she had felt earlier returned.

Given the few items used, they were done in a brief time.

"That's the last one," she said, handing him a plate. "I'm going."

"You know, I've been thinking all my plates could use a good washing." His gaze moved over the cabinets beside the stove and under the sink.

She tossed the dishrag into the sink. "Enough with your excuses to keep me here."

When he reached for her, she spun around and he touched nothing but air.

"Alexandra," he said to her back.

Her heart raced. A part of her wanted to respond, but the part of her that had shut down after Yuri's death held her still.

"Sasha," he said, "you know I'm afraid of you as much as you are of me."

That confession forced her to face him. "What do you have to fear from me?"

"How much I care about you. I'm worried that it clouds my judgment. I've always been…objective. My ex-wife used to say 'detached.' At least that's what she accused me of." He gave a slight sigh. "Maybe she was right. I'm not one to leave my work at the office."

"I guess I'm proof of that."

"You aren't work — anymore."

"Then what am I?"

He studied her for a moment. "Someone I care for very, very deeply."

This time, when he reached for her, she held her ground. As he stepped forward, her heart drummed against her ribs, and her breath came in quick pants. He touched his lips to hers. A simple, light brush. The defenses she'd built over the past months crumbled as a shudder crashed through her body, and a rush of emotions flooded her, leaving her demanding more.

She slid her wet fingers into his hair and tugged him closer as her lips parted to taste him. With an overpowering desire to truly touch him, she pulled his shirt from his pants and slipped her hands underneath it to stroke his taut muscles. He moaned into her mouth and shifted back to gaze into her eyes.

Without a word, she took his hand and led him to the bedroom.

At the door, he paused. "Are you sure?"

"Yes," she said with a bob of her head.

Backing away from him and into the room, she unfastened her skirt and let it drop. She watched his eyes follow her from her feet and legs, still covered in wool stockings, up her body to her face. Unable to return his gaze, she dropped hers to the buttons on her blouse. Slowly she unfastened them to reveal a wool undershirt. Her chest rose and fell, stretching the fabric across her breasts.

He moved to her and slipped the blouse off her shoulders, letting it fall to the floor. "Just how many layers do you have?"

"Only one more."

With his help, she pulled the undershirt over her head and then removed the stockings to reveal a pair of imported silk panties and matching bra.

When he raised his eyebrows, she blushed and said, "A gift from an old friend. Lena."

"I need to send her a thank-you note."

He took her in his arms. The rough fabric of his shirt grazed her skin. She pulled back.

"Did I do something wrong?" he asked.

"No, it's only..." She touched his shirt, reached over to the top button, and undid it. "It's a bit scratchy."

Soon, he stood before her clad only in a pair of briefs. She ran her hand over his chest with its sprinkling of hairs and smiled.

"What's so amusing?"

"Something someone once told me about hairy chests."

With one hand holding hers, he threw back the covers on the bed and then placed her in the center of the narrow bed. When he tried to lie down next to her, he slipped, almost falling off. Giggling, she moved closer to the wall, but still left only a little room for him.

"There's just one solution," he said with a broad grin.

He moved on top of her and buried his face in her hair, kissing it. "Sasha," he murmured again.

This time, the diminutive sent a thrill through her, matched only by the sparks his touch sent flying up and down her spine until she seemed to hum with anticipation. Using her fingers and mouth, she kissed, tasted, and explored him. Together, they learned each other's points of delight.

Her desire grew, pushing all thoughts from her mind until all that existed was that moment, Sergei's face, mouth, and hands. Her defenses gone, she yielded to his caresses.

Their joining became the last avenue to explore, and the final release left them both drained as they sank onto the bed.

Chapter Thirty-Four

Sergei cradled her cheek with his hand and stroked her face with his thumb. "Are you all right?" he asked, studying her eyes. "You look…sad."

Although she shook her head, she turned her back to him in the small bed. Matching the curve of her body with his own, he tugged her closer.

"This is…It's the first time…I've been…done…this…since Yuri died," she told the wall.

He held her loosely, enjoying her warmth against him. He kissed the back of her head. "You mean, you and Vladimir…?"

She stiffened at the mention of her former boss. After a moment, she shook her head, her hair caressing his lips as she did so.

"No. There was one night, but I couldn't."

"Would it help to know it's my first time since my divorce?"

She wiggled about to face him. "How long has that been?"

"Longer than most believe is healthy for a man."

Her gaze strayed past his face, and he could tell she focused on an object beyond him. She sat up, pushing him close to the edge of the bed. "I have to leave."

"Please. Stay. It's not safe."

"I can't hide out here."

"But you don't have to make yourself a visible target."

"What if Vladimir or Nikolai or the Iranians — whoever seems to be threatened by you — if they can't get to me and decide to go after Nadezhda? I have to find out who and why."

While he wanted to argue with her, her reasoning did make some sense. He let her crawl over him and gather her clothes. If he followed her, or had Pavel follow her, he might find out who. He shook his head to erase the thought of using her as bait.

Finally, he said, "At least let me give you a ride back to your apartment."

In the car, he considered various options of how to keep her safe. She didn't look at him, but kept gazing out the window. He had broken the most basic rule, getting involved. But there was no going back. Did she realize the change as much as he?

He broke the silence. "I want you to memorize some phone numbers."

"I have your card — "

"You might not be able to find it, or use it."

The rest of the trip, he made her repeat his home number, his office number, and Pavel's home number until he was certain she had them committed to memory.

A block from her apartment building, he directed the car to the curb. "It's probably best for you to walk from here. I'm going to arrange for you to be watched, but it will take a while. If you need me before that — "

"I know. Call you," she said, giving him a small, nervous smile.

He wanted to reach over, hold her, kiss her. Put the car in gear and drive away with her. Instead, he let his hand rest on hers for a moment. "Be careful… Sasha."

She took a deep breath, as if she were about to plunge under water, and opened the car door. After she stepped outside, she leaned over and spoke to him through the open door. "I will. If I find out more, I promise to call."

Chapter Thirty-Five

*T*he wind blasted into her face, forcing her to bow into it. Bits of snow from the drifts along the sidewalk stung her cheeks. She cursed herself for permitting Sergei to take her to his apartment. Had she forgotten so quickly that she'd decided to stop allowing others to control her? If only she hadn't felt vulnerable, and he hadn't seemed so solid, so commanding, she might not have fallen into that trap again. She appreciated his concern, but up to now, the only person who'd been attacked had been him. Better to call him as soon as she got to her apartment and tell him she didn't need his protection. If she found out anything, she'd let him know, but otherwise, no more contact with him.

With this plan in mind, she turned the corner into the courtyard of her apartment block with a firm, sure step. Almost immediately, she stopped, and her heart lurched. Across the snowy yard, she spied Vladimir's car parked just to one side of her entrance. The car straddled the sidewalk's curb, the tires on one side effectively blocking the walk. She pushed down the urge to run. If she were to be in control, she would have to confront him. Straightening her shoulders, she marched to the building.

"I was afraid I missed you," he said when she stepped onto the landing.

At least the new locks seemed to have worked.

"I must talk to you," he continued. "So much has happened."

"I was visiting Nadezhda. I need to talk to you too. Why

don't you come into the kitchen? We'll have some tea, then I have to get ready for work," she said, unlocking the door.

He followed her into the apartment. "That won't be necessary."

"Well, I'm a little hungry," she said, picking up the kettle from the stove.

She kept her back to him to hide her trembling hands.

"No, I mean you don't have to go to work." He stepped behind her and wrapped an arm about her waist. With all the willpower she could muster, she kept herself from flinching. "Remember how I promised you I would soon have enough money to take care of your problems? It's happened. I paid off Nikolai, just like I promised."

She turned to face him, her mouth open in surprise. "How did you get the money?"

"The deal with Ahmed. We completed it today."

Thoughts flew through her mind — the virus, the Iranians, Sergei. She forced a smile. "I'm so pleased for you. But I can't let you — "

"You had no problem asking me to help you a few days ago." The coldness in his voice made a shiver run down her spine. "Understand something. I paid Nikolai off. You owe *me* now — not him. I own you."

"*Own* me? In case you've forgotten, the Czar freed the serfs a hundred and fifty years ago."

He grabbed both of her arms, gripping her tightly. He looked into her eyes. "They know, Alexandra. Ahmed, Shirazi, they know you've been talking to the FSB."

"How do you — "

"Shh, my dear." He let go of one arm, and rubbed her cheek with his knuckles. "I'll protect you. I have protected you. The only reason you're not dead is because I promised to take you out of the country. I can't say the same about your friend. The Iranians might have succeeded today if you hadn't stepped in."

"But no one was there to save Kirov?" she asked and waited for his reaction.

His eyes widened, but whether out of surprise or amusement, she wasn't certain. Regardless, he didn't deny his role in the former administrator's death.

"He tried to cut me out. To sell his wares directly to the

Iranians instead of going through me. He would've still been selling off bits of stolen equipment for kopecks if it hadn't been for me. I would've given him his fair share, but he became greedy. People who try to cheat me don't live long."

Her whole body trembled at his veiled threat. As much as he vowed he loved her, she knew his tolerance had a limit. Considering her options, she decided to acquiesce. If she could make him relax, let down his guard, she might be able to call Sergei. "What are you planning to do now?"

"We're leaving the country. I have enough money now to set us up far away from here."

With great effort, she forced a smile and rasped out her response. "Where shall we go? Europe? I can't go without Nadezhda."

"Of course I expect you to bring your daughter. We'll go pick her up now."

"We? Now?"

"I don't plan to let you out of my sight. I warned you, not all my business partners agree with letting you live. We already have reservations on the flight to Moscow tonight. There, we switch planes to Turkey."

Her mind raced, trying to find some way to stall for time. To warn Sergei. "What about passports…and visas? We can't just leave the country."

With the indulgent smile one would give to a child, he pulled something out of his jacket breast pocket. "Your passports. Did you know Turkey and Sri Lanka do not require advanced visa applications for Russians? You simply obtain them at the airport. You see? I've thought of everything. I want you with me. Nothing is going to prevent me from having you this time."

"It will be…perfect," she whispered hoarsely.

He pulled her closer and kissed her, his tongue slipping into her mouth when she opened it in protest.

When he finally pulled back, she choked back a whimper. "I've never seen you like this."

"You have no idea how long I've waited for this moment," he said, brushing her hair from her forehead. "I've been patient, been a gentleman. No longer. I've learned to take what I want before someone else takes it from me. We go to pick up Nadezhda and then on to the airport."

"Let me just get her medicines," she said, pulling herself from his grasp. She rushed from the room and into her bedroom. In the doorway, her gaze stopped at the telephone on the nightstand. She could hear Sergei drilling her over the phone numbers.

Vladimir called from the hallway. "Alexandra?"

She pushed the urge to pick up the phone from her mind and pulled open the door of the storage cabinet above her closet. She grabbed the bottles there and tossed them into her purse, praying she would be able to find some way to get word to Sergei.

Chapter Thirty-Six

Sergei sat fuming in his car, mad at both himself and the traffic.

A long line of cars stretched in front of him, marking the route to headquarters. As soon as Alexandra had headed against the wind to her apartment, he knew it was time to get the politicians involved. He would turn the whole case over to Yevgeny; let him get all the glory, again. Gather up the files, call his supervisor, and step away now, tonight. Of course, he would do what he could to help her, arguing she had been an informant. Maybe even get her to Moscow where her daughter might get better care.

For the moment, however, he was stuck in a queue longer than the worst bread lines. Red and blue lights flashed in the distance, signaling a major accident least half a kilometer ahead. Nothing to do but wait. As soon as he could get out of this mess, he would call Pavel and have him watch Alexandra.

He watched with envy the cars coming from the opposite direction, their headlights reflecting off the icy roadway. Like many Russian cities, this one had a river passing through its center, and the road he was on wound itself along the riverbank. To his right, the water glistened white below a steep embankment. To his left, the oncoming traffic effectively blocked any course other than the one that inched forward before him.

For the most part, the drivers in the other cars seemed accepting of the situation. No honking or angry gesturing. Simply shuffling forward with the same fatalistic tolerance shown in other lines. The queue was a basic ingredient of Russian life — for food, for buses, everything. Russians had long ago learned to retreat within themselves and practice the long-suffering patience developed over generations.

In the end, he was no different. Finally resigning himself to the current situation, he let his mind drift back to that afternoon. Her warmth, her softness, the hunger in both of them. Lost in these thoughts, he didn't notice the car coming in the opposite direction until it slowed down almost to a stop, and he had no time to react before a gun flashed through the car's open window.

Chapter Thirty-Seven

All the way to her in-laws' apartment, Alexandra sought some way to warn Sergei. The only phone at her in-laws' was in the living room. If she could get them to sit in the kitchen…or perhaps she could convince Vladimir to drop her at her apartment afterward to pack.

She also worried about leaving Yuri's parents. Should anything go wrong, they could become targets for revenge or blackmail. During the Soviet period, citizens traveling abroad had to leave their families behind. Insurance against their return. Few would consider defecting if their family at home would suffer as a result. She wanted to be certain the same wouldn't happen to hers.

Vladimir broke into her thoughts when he placed a hand on her thigh and rubbed it lightly. Her stomach contracted. Recalling the rough, possessive kiss he'd given her earlier, she willed herself not to shove the hand away.

"What are you thinking about, my dear?" he asked, glancing in her direction.

"Trying to decide what to pack. Turkey must be warm this time of year."

"Don't worry about packing. We'll buy new things there."

"Also, I was thinking perhaps Ivan and Katerina could come with us? At least temporarily. They're used to taking care of Nadezhda, and it would give me more time to spend with you."

She placed her hand over his, and he grasped it. "I'll think about it. I'm not evil. You know that. We've known each other almost all our lives."

"Yes. There were times…"

"And those times can be ours again, if you let them."

"Of course." With a smile, she squeezed his hand, but continued to stare out the window at the passing street scenes, afraid her eyes would betray her.

❧

Nadezhda greeted them at the door, a great smile on her face. Immediately taking her mother's hand, she chattered away about something on television, ending with, "*Dyedushka* says they are not real. Are they, Mommy?"

"No, I'm afraid they're not," she said, stepping inside with Vladimir.

"They're make-believe, just like the stories you sometimes tell me."

"*Dyedushka* was right?" she asked.

"Yes, he was," she said, giving her daughter a pat on the head. Shifting her gaze, she stared into her father-in-law's eyes as he stepped into view. "Your grandfather is a very wise man."

"Two visits so quickly together," Ivan said, stepping forward to greet her and Vladimir. "I hope everything's all right."

Katerina arrived from the kitchen. The moment her gaze settled on Vladimir, her smile shifted slightly.

"I have good news," Alexandra said with more than a little forced enthusiasm. "Vladimir has invited all of us on holiday to Turkey."

"Such a generous offer," Ivan said. "I don't know what to say."

Katerina's spine stiffened slightly. "I do. Thank you, but it is too generous. We can't accept."

"I only asked you for Alexandra's sake." The muscles in Vladimir's face tightened. "We're leaving tonight and came to get Nadezhda and her things."

Alexandra's heart fluttered. "Wait, please, let's talk about this for a moment. They're just surprised. To have an offer like this come out of the blue…"

"No time for discussions. I have some things to do. We — "

Nadezhda pulled on her skirt. "Mommy, what's Turkey?"

"It's another country, very far away," she said, kneeling down to meet her daughter eye to eye. "We're going on holiday. In an

177

airplane. To the beach."

"What's a beach?"

"A place with lots and lots of sand."

"I know all about sand. There's a sand box outside in the yard, but you can't see it now. It's covered with snow."

"But that is just a little bit of sand. Imagine a sandbox as big and wide as a road that goes as far as you can see. That's a beach. And it's warm there. No snow. Ever."

The little girl drew in her breath, her face brightening with delight and wonder. "Sand? And no snow? I want to go."

"We will."

"Come on," said Vladimir.

He opened the small closet next to the front door and removed Nadezhda's coat and boots.

"But *Dyedushka* and *Babuskha* don't want to come with us?" Nadezhda turned to her grandparents. "Please. You can play in the sand with me."

Katerina's face contorted as she appeared to be searching for the right excuse to give her granddaughter.

Ivan crouched down next to Nadezhda after exchanging glances with her mother. "We're not like you, poppit. We're too old just to drop everything and come right away. We need time to pack." He glanced up at Vladimir. "Perhaps we could join you in a few days?"

"I don't know how long we will be there," he said, annoyance shading his voice. "I have plans to travel on after we get to Turkey."

"To where?" asked Katerina. "This doesn't sound like a holiday."

"I don't plan to return."

"At least let them know where we'll be at first. So they can join us, if they decide," Alexandra said.

After a moment's hesitation, he said, "The Grand Hotel in Antalya." He glanced down at Nadezhda and said generously, "Right on the beach. For you."

"The beach! The beach! Let's go," she said, grabbing her mother's hand and dragging her toward the bedroom. "Let's get my things. I can't wait."

She allowed her daughter to pull her along just as the situation seemed to be overpowering her options as well.

Chapter Thirty-Eight

Sergei's left arm burned. He tried to reach over to check it with his right, but found he couldn't move that one either. After cracking open his eyes, he shut them as quickly. Nothing made sense. Bright lights and buzzing voices surrounded him. He gasped as memories flooded his consciousness. The gun flash, the car window exploding, and the pain in his arm. Only when the bloodstain seeped through the layers of his coat did he realize he'd been shot. Jerking the wheel with his good arm, he'd crossed the yellow line and pulled into the path of oncoming traffic. He'd dodged the cars coming toward him and steered the car straight toward the police vehicles and the three-car pileup that had stopped traffic and left him a sitting duck.

With a grunt, he forced his eyes open and attempted to sit up, but something restrained him. Checking around, he found he was strapped to a hospital gurney. A bare bulb hanging from a wire overhead glared into his face.

"You were lucky," a voice said from the foot of the gurney. Pavel frowned at him. "It missed anything vital, but you lost blood. The traffic…"

Sergei opened his eyes wider, seeking clues to what had happened when he'd stumbled from his car. Several glass bottles hung from an apparatus resembling a wire coat rack. Tubes led from the bottles into his good arm, which was strapped to a metal bed rail. His other arm was bandaged from the shoulder to just below the elbow. He was in a hospital hallway, shuttled to one side to allow others to pass.

As if in response to his observations, Pavel said, "They're waiting for a room. You just came out of surgery."

"How long?" he asked. His throat was raw, and his voice raspy.

"You've been here about two hours. I would guess about three hours since they shot at you." He dropped his gaze.

"What is it?"

"Yevgeny's taken over the case. I had to tell them everything. Vladimir has the girl and her daughter and appears to be leaving the country."

"How could you?" Sergei shifted, but the straps held him down. The whole gurney bucked and swayed precariously.

Pavel grabbed hold of the stretcher's foot to keep it from tipping over.

"Hold still. There's more." Sergei quit thrashing. "They've taken her in-laws to headquarters for questioning."

"All this in three hours? That fool Yevgeny's going to ruin everything. I've got to get out of here. Help me."

He swung his injured arm at the straps holding down his right. A jolt of pain radiated from his arm to his whole body. He settled back, nausea sweeping over him.

"You can't go anywhere," Pavel said. "You've just been shot."

"If I don't go, the virus is going to get out of this country, and we'll all pay the price. Now help me pull this thing out of my arm."

Pavel glanced up and down the hallway. With a look of helplessness, he moved to Sergei's side and released his good arm. He studied the needle sticking out of it and blanched. "I have no idea how to…"

"Just give it a quick yank."

Sergei braced himself as Pavel reached for the place where the tube and needle met, then swung his left arm over to press his fingers over the needle's hole. "Now help me sit up."

Pavel checked about him before assisting his superior into an upright position.

His head spun for a moment along with another wave of nausea, then cleared. Only then did he realize he was naked except for a thin cotton gown.

"Damn. Where are my clothes? Give me your coat and trousers." Pavel's eyes widened. "You heard me. I have to get to the office before Yevgeny destroys any hope of us stopping the virus."

After a moment's hesitation, Pavel pulled down his pants to reveal a pair of briefs emblazoned with scarlet hearts. His face turned a deeper color than the underwear's decoration. "They were a gift from my wife."

"Wrap up in this sheet," his boss said and swung his legs over the side of the gurney.

"You there, what's going on?" A nurse built like the Kremlin's wall ran toward them, her heavy steps echoing down the hallway. "You can't leave like this."

Despite the slight sway in his stance, Sergei shoved his legs into the pants. They were too short and too tight in the middle for him to fasten, but his hips held them in place. He signaled Pavel to hand him his coat. When he tried to put his left arm into the sleeve, the pain convinced him to just drape it over his shoulder on that side.

The nurse had reached them and was explaining in a voice loud enough to attract the attention of others about hospital rules. Sergei ignored her as he checked the coat pockets and drew out a set of keys.

"Where's the car parked?" he asked Pavel over the nurse's protests.

With one hand clutched about his makeshift toga, Pavel raised his hand to flash his credentials and stop the nurse's harangue. "FSB. Please come with me."

The sight of the badge silenced her.

Pavel turned to his boss. "In the lot to the left."

The younger agent led her away from Sergei and cut off a group of hospital employees responding to her cries.

After the first few steps, Sergei paused and leaned against the wall to catch his breath. Checking on Pavel, he saw the agent had calmed the assembled staff and dispersed them. He smiled. The man had potential.

The trip to the front door took him longer than he'd hoped. He had to lean against the wall two more times to keep from falling, but he'd gained strength by the time he reached the door. The cold concrete made him realize he had forgotten to take

Pavel's shoes.

"Want these?" Pavel asked behind him.

He held up Sergei's boots in one hand and clenched his boss's pants about his waist with the other. "If you'd just waited a few minutes, we could have left better prepared."

With a grimace, Sergei grabbed his boots and shoved his feet in them. "You'd better drive. I'm not sure about shifting and steering at the same time."

❧

Sergei and Pavel ignored the stares they caused as they passed through the first floor of FSB headquarters and took the stairs to the interrogation rooms. That area was everything the Western movies depicted them to be. Below ground. Cinderblock walls with peeling gray paint. Dim lighting that could be complemented with a bright spotlight, if needed. Yevgeny paced the hallway between the two chambers. He glared at Sergei when the two stepped in sight.

"Tell me what you've done," Sergei said. "I need to see how we can salvage this."

"What I've done?" Yevgeny's flushed. "It's what you've done that requires explanation. Unauthorized surveillance, removal of classified documents, fraternizing with suspects…"

"Just how much did you tell him?" Sergei asked Pavel.

His assistant gave a helpless shrug. "He's my commander."

"And as commander, I've taken over this investigation." Yevgeny waved his hand at Sergei. "You've created enough problems. I have everything under control. The suspects will be stopped at the airport and searched. If they have the virus, we'll know it. I have two other accomplices in interrogation now. They were packing, preparing to flee the country. We'll destroy this whole operation shortly."

"You'll destroy things, all right." Blood drained from his head, making it swim. "Your ignorance will ruin months of work. There's no 'operation.' Just a business deal. A one-time sale. And we have to stop it before it's completed."

"We will stop it. I have a microbiologist who worked in a bioweapons institute in there. Just like you've said all along, they're the ones to watch. All we have to do is find out what he knows about the virus, and we end it. I wouldn't be surprised if he was the mastermind of a whole network…"

When Sergei raised his arms in desperation, he swayed on his feet. Pavel grabbed his good shoulder to steady him. "What you've got in there is an old man who only wants to live out his retirement in peace. I'm talking to them."

He pushed past Yevgeny and entered the first interrogation room. Katerina sat behind a metal table, her arms crossed under her breasts and her short, curled hair disheveled. With a wave at the agents in the room, Sergei shooed them out and slumped into a chair opposite her.

"What's happened to Alexandra and Nadezhda?"

"I've already told them. I know nothing. I'm just a grandmother who has been retired since my fifty-fifth birthday." She jabbed her chin at the door. "They kept asking me about my work at the Institute. I tried to tell them I may have worked in there, but all I did was clean — "

"I don't care about what you did ten years ago. I need to know what's happening now. Where's Alexandra."

"You think I'd tell you anything? Go ahead, threaten me. I don't scare easily. My mother survived the Siege of Leningrad. She was sixteen. Her duty was to collect the corpses of those who died the night before. My bedtime stories were about those nine hundred days of war and starvation."

Sergei leaned forward in the chair, resting his good arm on the table. "I'm not asking you to betray Alexandra. I need to find Vladimir. He's got something that could kill more people than the eight hundred thousand who died in Leningrad during the siege. Where is he?"

"That man is up to no good," she said with a sniff. "Throwing his money and his father's influence around. With Yuri barely cold in the grave, he takes her on holiday with him. I say good riddance."

"And Nadezhda too? You'd say good riddance to her?"

"My little angel." Her composure gone, she buried her head in her hands and sobbed. "The only thing left of my poor Yuri."

"Then tell me where they're going. We may still be able to stop them."

"He said something about Turkey. I don't remember any more." Raising her head, she said, "Ivan. Ivan asked for the name of the hotel."

Sergei stood, holding onto the table for support and patted her on her shoulder. "Thank you. I'm going to try to save both of them."

"Let her go," he told the two agents smoking in the hallway when he stepped from the room.

Yevgeny stomped toward him. "Just a moment. I know for a fact — "

"You know nothing. And neither does she. I'm talking to the man."

His energy and adrenaline waning, he stumbled as he passed his superior. Yevgeny caught him by his bad arm, and he yelped.

"Go back to the hospital and stay there," Yevgeny said. "It'll be the last thing the agency will cover for you."

With a grimace, Sergei jerked his arm free. "At least I won't have to explain how my incompetence let a deadly virus out of the country."

The two men faced each other. Despite Sergei's debilitated state, Yevgeny glanced away first. "Go ahead." He waved a dismissive hand. "Make a fool of yourself. You'll get nothing from him."

Sergei gave him a curt bow, turned to the two agents still smoking behind him, and grabbed the pack of cigarettes from one's pocket. As an afterthought, he also pulled the lighter from the officer's hand. After winking at the surprised man, he marched into the second interrogation room.

Ivan's stance mirrored Katerina's — stoic silence. Again, Sergei shooed the agents from the room and dropped wearily in a chair. He took a cigarette from the pack. Not his brand, but at the moment, it didn't matter. He offered one to Ivan, but the man declined with a shake of his head.

"I'm terribly sorry for all this." Sergei blew a cloud toward the ceiling. "None of this would have happened, if I hadn't been…temporarily indisposed."

Ivan's gaze dropped to Sergei's arm where Pavel's coat still partially hid the bandages.

"We need to know about Alexandra," he said. "She's in danger. The same people who tried to kill me may be after her."

"She's gone away. She'll be safe."

"It's the person she's with who concerns me. Morozov — "

"I've known Vladimir all his life, and his father is a member of Parliament. Are you questioning their loyalty to the Motherland? Or mine? I have served our country for the past thirty years…"

"I know you're a patriot. Decorated with special honors. Your son too." At the mention of Yuri, Ivan's gaze shot to Sergei's face. "If the Union hadn't fallen, who knows what he might have achieved. But some things are more important than our own welfare, and Vladimir's stepped over the line. You know what he's got, don't you? Maybe you didn't when Alexandra spoke to you, but perhaps a few calls told you everything?"

Ivan's eyes narrowed as he studied him. "You're the FSB agent who told her about her father, aren't you?"

Sergei shrugged. Pain shot through this shoulder and the upper half of his body. "I thought it might help her understand the dangers. And she is in danger. You know he has the virus with him." He leveled his stare on Ivan. "Katerina said he mentioned Turkey."

"That woman always did talk too much." Ivan pointed at the cigarette pack. Sergei gave it to him, and he took a moment to light one, inhaling the smoke slowly. "They're supposed to fly to Antalya."

Using the table for balance, Sergei pushed himself to a standing position. "Thank you."

Ivan reached into his breast pocket and passed a piece of paper across to him. "The hotel where they'll be staying. Please, save them. They're the only family we have left."

He nodded, and with a slightly faltering step, returned to the shadowy hallway to find it deserted, except for Pavel. Somehow the other man had gotten a belt and managed to gather Sergei's pants about his waist.

"We need to get to the airport; we may be able to stop this — " Sergei said.

"Yevgeny got a call." Pavel shook his head. "They searched them at the airport and found nothing. They've let them go."

"Go?" His head pounded when he shouted the word. "That fool has just signed the export license."

"There's still a chance to stop them in Moscow," Pavel said. "They'll have to change airports, and…"

"Good thinking." Cold perspiration beaded Sergei's upper lip. He shivered and pulled the coat about him tighter. "We'll get to Moscow and…"

He leaned against the wall and slid to a crouched position.

"You're not going anywhere," Pavel said. "I'll go."

"Then I need to give you a name," he said, feeling lightheaded. "He can help find out which flight to Antalya. Tell him to take care of Alexandra for me."

"Of course," Pavel said.

At least, that's what Sergei thought he said. He never heard the words, just read his lips. Darkness closed about him. Through the fog, he repeated Marcus's name and number, hoping Pavel could understand.

Chapter Thirty-Nine

The knot in Alexandra's stomach, formed when she saw Vladimir's car in front of her apartment building, pulled itself tighter when the taxi stopped in front of the airport. The last time she'd been there, Vladimir had picked her up from her trip to Moscow, and Yuri had been slipping the noose around his neck. She swallowed hard, gripped Nadezhda's hand, and stepped onto the sidewalk. The driver jumped out and hauled two suitcases from the trunk. Peeling some bills off a roll he pulled from his pocket, Vladimir paid him, and one of the stubble-faced men lounging on a rickety cart sauntered forward to collect the bags from the curb.

Once the luggage was on the cart, Vladimir opened one and pulled a stuffed bear from it. Nadezhda's eyes widened at its sight. "Is that for me?"

"Yes, for you, little hope." He knelt down on one knee, appearing almost paternal. His voice took on a very serious tone. "I want you to take good care of it."

"I will, I will," she said, imitating his grave face and carefully cradling the bear in her arms.

"Let's go," he said, straightening from the crouch and grasping Alexandra's arm.

He motioned to the baggage handler to follow them inside and marched Alexandra and Nadezhda toward the check-in counters. A series of wooden booths with electronic boards overhead displaying a number and destination directed passengers where to check in for a particular flight. Although most of the booths were dark and empty, one marked for Moscow had a long line snaking from it. A young woman stood behind the counter, exchanging boarding passes for tickets. Passengers passed bags through an opening at the bottom of the booth to a man in a faded jumpsuit who weighed and checked each piece.

Ignoring the line, Vladimir strode straight to the front and directed the man pushing the luggage cart to place their bags inside the booth.

"These people were already waiting," Alexandra whispered to him, feeling the other passengers' glares on them. "Don't you think we should go to the end of the line?"

"Nonsense," he said in a loud voice. "First-class passengers are supposed to have priority. Besides, we're traveling with a sick child."

The tired-looking woman behind the counter didn't seem to care either. She simply took the tickets and passports he handed her, studied them for a moment, and struck them with her stamp.

As she handed them back to Vladimir, the gray-jacketed arm of a police officer reached from behind him and snatched the tickets. "One moment, please."

Pushing his hat back on his forehead, the policeman studied the tickets, spoke into a radio attached to his right shoulder, and turned to them when a voice crackled orders back. "Follow me, please."

Vladimir maintained his arrogant calm with an almost amused air about him. They followed the officer through the dreary departure area to a door at the far end. Another officer opened the door, scrutinized the three, and motioned for them to enter.

The office could barely contain the desk and chair furnishing the room, let alone three additional people. Cigarette smoke filled the small space, and the commanding officer glared at them from behind the blue cloud.

Before either he or Vladimir could exchange words, someone knocked again, and the first policeman shoved a cart with their baggage into the small space, forcing them into the back wall. After the door closed, the officer helped himself to another cigarette and flipped through the documents the policeman had taken from them at the gate.

After several minutes, the man glared up at them. "Open your bags." He pointed to the briefcase Vladimir carried. "Start with that one."

"Certainly."

With an amiable smile, Vladimir placed the briefcase on the desk and flipped the latch open to reveal a few papers. The officer riffled through the papers and ran his hand over the case. When he was through, Vladimir closed the case with a snap and pulled a bag from the cart and flipped its latch, exposing the few things Alexandra had gathered for Nadezhda from her grandparents' house. Once again the officer ran his hands around the sides of the bag and through its contents.

"Stop him," Nadezhda said with a whimper. "Stop that bad man from breaking my things."

When Alexandra picked up the child, trying to soothe her, the commander glowered at the two of them and waved his hand. "Take her outside. I can't abide the noise."

Gratefully, she obeyed. Once in the departure hall, another officer detained her just outside the door. She held the little girl and paced in front of the door. She glanced at the man guarding her. After all of Sergei's warnings, she wasn't sure whom to trust. Her one hope was that they would find the virus. At least if they were arrested she might be able to have them contact Sergei.

All too quickly, however, she knew her prayer had not been answered. The commander and Vladimir stepped into the hallway.

The officer signaled to all of them. "Follow me."

They marched in a line across the hallway — the commander, Vladimir, Alexandra and Nadezhda, and finally the policeman pushing the cart with their baggage. Stopping at an unmarked door at the end of the line of check-in booths, the commander rapped sharply. The door creaked open to reveal an ancient baggage X-ray machine. Motioning to Vladimir to push the cart through the door, he spoke to two people sitting on the machine. "Scan the bags and them."

After positioning himself next to the technician at the machine's monitor, the commander motioned at Vladimir to place the first bag on the dusty conveyor belt. Alexandra, still holding her daughter and the new stuffed animal, watched the bag jerk forward and into the machine. The officer and the technician stared intently at the glowing screen. The process was repeated with all their baggage and hand luggage.

The commander returned to Vladimir and handed him the tickets and other documents. "Sorry for the inconvenience," he said with a grumble. "You may return to the ticket counter and complete your check-in."

"Thank you."

Vladimir took their papers and, without another word, turned on his heel. They returned to the booth, his hand firmly gripping Alexandra's elbow.

What had they expected to find? Vladimir hadn't even had a large amount of money. Alexandra raised her head and studied the baggage as each piece slid back through the slot at the bottom of the booth. No money meant he hadn't exchanged the virus yet. It still had to be on him. But where?

Given the late hour, Alexandra had hoped Nadezhda would sleep throughout the flight to Moscow. She needed time to think, to plan some way of keeping Vladimir from taking the virus out of the country. The little girl, however, didn't cooperate. She chattered constantly, striking up conversations with the flight attendants and insisting her mother sing with her. Although she prevented Alexandra from thinking, she also served as the best chaperone possible. Despite his own efforts to convince Nadezhda to sleep, Vladimir finally quit trying to make any physical advances during the flight. Each time he would reach for Alexandra, the little girl would invent a new game or request another song.

As soon as the plane landed and the passengers gave their customary applause for having arrived in one piece, Vladimir was up and out of his seat. With the plane still taxiing down the tarmac, he insisted they move to the front. The moment the ground crew had the mobile stairs at the door and the hatch opened, he shoved Alexandra and Nadezhda onto the gangway outside into the early Moscow morning.

"What's all the rush?" she asked, as he insisted on carrying Nadezhda to move them faster across the tarmac. "We still have to wait for the bags."

"I've arranged for someone to pick up the bags and meet us at Sheremetyevo," he said, possessing her elbow once again. "There's some business I have to do before we get on the plane. I have a car waiting."

She glanced around her, seeking a possible escape route if he ever lowered his guard. More than one plane was unloading passengers. She might be able to slip in with them, but Vladimir held Nadezhda. She couldn't leave without her.

As if he had read her mind, he squeezed her arm and increased his pace. She ducked her head and followed him inside the terminal.

Passing onto the street, Vladimir signaled to a waiting car. Having learned from the plane ride, she strategically placed her daughter on the seat between them, but to her dismay, the child yawned twice, put her head on her mother's lap and immediately fell asleep. Holding her breath, she awaited Vladimir's attention, but he turned his interest to the streets, staring intently out his side window as if searching for something, or someone.

Moscow's four major airports were located at different corners of the city and serviced different parts of the country. They had arrived at Domodedovo airport in the southeast, used mostly by planes from Siberia and points further east. Sheremetyevo, the international airport built for the 1980 Olympics, lay almost exactly kitty-corner to Domodedovo, requiring a drive through town and the morning commuter traffic. Unlike Siberia, Moscow was experiencing an early spring warming. Restaurants had already set up outdoor seating in front of their establishments. Although they still had to wear light coats, many Muscovites were willing to brave the chill to catch a bit of sun while enjoying coffee or tea.

Reaching the center of the city, Vladimir leaned forward and spoke to the driver. At one such café, the car slowed to a stop by the curb. Vladimir got out and turned to offer his hand to Alexandra.

She glanced at his extended hand. "What are we doing here?"

"I thought it might be nice to have something to drink before we got to the airport," he said with a brief smile. "We have plenty of time."

She hesitated a moment longer. A number of young men and women sat the tables with their drinks — safe enough. After she gathered Nadezhda in her arms, he grasped her forearm and helped her out into the crisp daylight.

When he had helped her take a seat at an empty table, he waved to a passing waiter and ordered coffees for both of them.

He sipped his when it arrived and glared at her. "You're not thirsty?"

With a shake of her head, she shifted Nadezhda on her lap so the child's head rested on her chest and said, "It's too hot. I'm letting it cool."

"Why do you have to defy me?"

"What difference does it make to you whether I drink it or not? I'm here. With you. You have what you want."

"I want you to be grateful. I saved you. If it weren't for me, you'd be dead by now. Just like your FSB friend." She stared at him, and a smile curled wickedly across his face. "That's right. They shot him just before we left."

Her heart sank. Sergei, her last chance of escape, was gone. Reaching for the coffee, she realized her hand shook and stopped, dropping it onto the table.

"Don't be frightened." He placed his hand over hers. "Do you see now how much I love you? The risk I'm taking? I've waited too long. You're mine, and I'm going to have you, the whole world be damned."

He leaned forward suddenly and placed his lips over hers. As before, he forced his tongue into her mouth. Tears stung her eyes as she closed them and submitted to his touch. He placed his hand on the back of her neck and pulled her head closer to him. Forcing herself to yield to him, she shut off any thoughts of rescue. Her only chance would come if he relaxed his vigilance.

"Is this what you're going to be like from now on?" she asked, her voice shaking when he had finished. "One of the things I always admired about you was that you were always a gentleman."

"Maybe being a gentleman was part of my problem. I didn't want your admiration. I wanted you."

Raising his gaze, he met hers. "See the others sitting at this café and on the street here? They're the ones taking advantage of the changes and making money from it. The rest are poor dupes who believe the government will come through in the end and take care of them." He leaned back again in his seat and sipped his coffee. "You can't depend on anyone but yourself in these times. That was Yuri's mistake. He depended too much on others. He believed he could trust those who lent him money. 'Trust no one and believe in no one but yourself ' has served me well."

Despite the warm breeze, she shivered as his words touched

home. "Does that include me? Do you trust me?"

"To a point. Do you know how long I've loved you? Or how difficult it was for me to think of you with Yuri? But I knew if I were patient, he'd ruin things. He did, and now I have you." He leaned forward, and she feared he would kiss her again. Instead, he simply stroked Nadezhda's head. She stirred slightly. "I'm so glad she looks like you. In time, I'm sure I'll be able to love her too."

After a check up and down the street, he stood, tossed several large ruble bills onto the table, and said, "Let's go. We need to get to the airport."

By the time she rose from her chair and had adjusted Nadezhda's head on her shoulder, Vladimir was already tapping his foot beside the open car door. She turned to step into the back seat and caught a glimpse of a familiar figure further down the street. Pausing, she watched Ahmed turn and hurry in the opposite direction.

Out of the corner of her eye, she saw Vladimir's facial muscles tighten. "Get in."

The rest of the way to the airport, he glared out the window and drummed his fingers on the briefcase in his lap.

His sour mood continued at Sheremetyevo. He dismissed the driver without a word and stepped onto the sidewalk with her and Nadezhda still clasped to his side.

Again, she dismissed the idea of trying to escape when she saw how little room she'd have to run from him in the crowded terminal.

The airport was built to accommodate far less flights than it currently serviced. People were everywhere. Arriving and departing passengers pushed their way in or out. A group of men in ill-fitting jumpsuits lounged on bent metal carts underneath a cloud of cigarette smoke, waiting for someone to offer them a few rubles to wheel their bags inside. Men in dark leather jackets, black fur hats, and two-days' stubble offered their services as taxi drivers to all who passed.

After a brief search of the men with the carts, Vladimir spotted their bags on one and waved him forward. Using the cart as a battering ram, the baggage handler plowed forward through the terminal to an opening in the waist-high tubing separating the check-in counters from the main terminal. Just as he had at the first airport, Vladimir ignored the other passengers' irritated stares as he followed the man to the front of the queue where a pair of security guards waited to check exit documents and X-ray each passenger's bags before allowing the person to pass.

This review was much more perfunctory than the one they had received on the earlier flight. All too soon for Alexandra, they had their boarding passes and made it through passport review. She could feel her chances of discovering Vladimir's plans or escaping from him narrowing. Not that it mattered anymore. Without Sergei, even if she knew where Vladimir had the virus, she had no one she could trust with the information.

Passing through passport control renewed Vladimir's spirits. With a smile, he said, "Let's celebrate our departure."

After studying the various restaurants on the second level overlooking the departure gates, he pointed to one bar at a corner above some of the brightly lit, duty-free kiosks. "We'll go there. We can see our gate from that one. You must be tired of carrying Nadezhda. Give her to me. We need to think of ourselves as a family, and I should begin to be her father."

With some reluctance, she placed Nadezhda in his outstretched arms. He cradled her, her head resting on his shoulder, and tucked the teddy bear under his arm.

At the bar, he ordered a gin and tonic for himself and an orange juice for her. After trying to drink with one hand and supporting the child with the other, he smiled. "Guess I need more practice. You hold her."

They rearranged themselves so Nadezhda lay partly on her mother's lap and partly on a chair. Despite one wall of windows opening onto the tarmac, the departure hall remained dark and gloomy. Brown rings, designed to imitate those from the Olympic Games, covered the ceiling. Heavy wood paneling and dull black tiles gave it an overall sinister atmosphere, reinforcing her own despair.

"It's no use," Vladimir said, as if he could read her mind.

"Excuse me?"

"You're not going to find a way to leave me."

"I wasn't – "

"You've been searching for an escape ever since we went to your in-laws. I told you, you're mine now. Accept it."

"I'm going to take a walk." He stood and stretched. "I want to check the duty-free. Maybe I'll buy you a little something for the trip. Wait here. Others are watching, and they have orders to not let you leave the airport."

With a pat on her hand, he left her, whistling through his teeth.

Alone, she used her vantage point from the bar's balcony to follow his stroll through the neon-lighted duty-free kiosks. After examining the bottles displayed at one perfume counter almost directly below her, he turned and sauntered into the main duty-free store further down the hall. She lost sight of him inside the store and leaned over the rail to see if he left through another exit. Out of the corner of her eye, she saw a man seated two tables down lean forward as well. Settling back in her seat, she sensed he had done likewise. Was he watching her, as Vladimir had warned?

A voice over the loudspeaker announced their flight to Turkey. Across the hallway, those in the boarding area lined up in front of the gangway. She scanned the floor below, seeking a glimpse of Vladimir, but couldn't find him. Was this part of his plan? To leave her in the airport as some sort of a distraction?

By the time they announced the final boarding call for their flight, her heart was beating furiously. He must have left her. As she frantically searched the terminal without catching sight of him, she considered her options. If she remained at the bar and let the plane leave without her, her life and Nadezhda's were in danger. She could try to leave the airport with the hope Vladimir had lied about her being watched. Or she could get on the plane and leave. Once out of the country, she might be able to contact Lena and get to the US. Another announcement about the flight's departure boomed across the terminal.

After a final moment's hesitation, she gathered Nadezhda in her arms and stepped toward the stairs. Hearing a set of footsteps behind her, she quickened her step. When she reached the stairs, someone grabbed her arm from behind and spun her around. She stared into Vladimir's eyes.

"Where do you think you're going?"

Her mind raced. Where had he come from? Glancing behind him, she caught sight of a second staircase on the far side of the balcony.

"I-I…the plane," she said.

"Anxious to being our holiday? I'm so glad." He pulled her close and gave her a quick peck on the lips. "Sorry to have kept you waiting, but business called."

As they descended the slippery stone steps, she asked, "You finished your business?"

"Quite profitably."

She studied the far end of the terminal, hoping to catch a glimpse of Ahmed.

"Nothing to see, my dear. And even if you did, who would you tell? Let's go; they're calling us again."

The descent awakened Nadezhda. At the bottom of the stairs, she grumpily wiped her eyes and yawned. "My bear. Where's my new bear?" she asked.

Alexandra searched among the things she carried. "I don't know. We must've left it somewhere. Maybe it's still at the table?"

"I want my bear!"

Her wails attracted the attention of everyone around them. Alexandra checked their gate and could see the crew pacing about, obviously waiting for them to board. Imagining Nadezhda crying for the whole flight to Turkey, she put the child down and spun around to return to the table.

"Where are you going?" Vladimir asked.

"Back to the bar. The bear must be there. Go on to the plane. I'll meet you there."

"No. I'll buy another bear. She'll be all right."

"It'll just take a minute," she said.

Glancing toward the gate, she saw an attendant checking her watch. "Tell them I'll be there."

Without her burdens, she moved quickly up the stairs. Vladimir dropped his briefcase next to her bag and followed, dragging a howling Nadezhda with him.

"Come with me now," he said, grabbing Alexandra's arm when she reached the top of the stairs.

"You want her to cry like this all the way to Turkey? I'm only going to see if it's at the table."

"It's not there. Now get on the plane."

She faced him, their eyes level. Nadezhda squirmed in his tightening grip. With a sudden rush of insight, she understood it all.

"There's no bear because you left it with Ahmed."

"Come with me now."

Anger welled inside her and overwhelmed her fear. Without any conscious thought, her arm swung up from her side, and she slapped him across the face.

"You beast! You used Nadezhda to carry that tube of death?"

Her arm flew to hit him again, but this time he grabbed it with his free arm. The movement threw them all off balance, and Vladimir slipped backward on the stairs, dragging both her and Nadezhda with him. Alexandra seized Nadezhda's free arm and flailed at the handrail running down the middle of the staircase. The child yelped as Alexandra tightened her hold on her daughter's arm and the rail. Vladimir's fingers slid from Nadezhda's hand, and he tumbled further down the stairs before he, too, stopped himself by gripping the rail.

Hauling herself to her feet, she righted Nadezhda, now whimpering softly and rubbing her arm. But Vladimir had also gotten to his feet. Grabbing her daughter, she took several steps up the stairs and froze. The burly man from the bar blocked their path.

"Alexandra," he mouthed, more than said aloud.

Her heart drummed in her chest. They must have sent him. She took a step sideways, crossed under the handrail, and descended on the other side, pulling Nadezhda behind her. As they passed Vladimir, he reached under the handrail and snared the child's hand. He jerked hard, and Nadezhda slipped from Alexandra's grasp.

Before she could spin around, the child squealed.

Once she did turn back, ready to continue the fight, the scene in front of her froze her in her tracks. Vladimir held Nadezhda by one foot, dangling her over the side of the stairs. At two-thirds of the way up the staircase, her head hung almost two stories from the black stone tiles below.

The whole terminal grew silent. The only noise was the child's whimpers. "Mommy?"

"It's all right," she called out to her. "I'm coming."

In slow, deliberate movements, she ducked under the handrail and took a step up the stairs, never taking her eyes off Vladimir. "Please. Let her go."

"I told you I'd buy her another one." He took a step backward. "Why couldn't you do what I asked? You always have to make me do things I don't want to."

She kept her gaze on him, afraid to glance at her daughter, and ascended one step. "Like turning Yuri in to the police?"

His expression shifted to one of surprise. "You knew? He was going to make you quit working. I had to keep you near me. I thought if he lost the car parts…"

"I see that now. You didn't know he would commit suicide." She took another step, but so did he.

"You realize I've done it all for you? The company, this deal. I've wanted you for so long, ever since graduation."

"Yes, I understand." Another step.

Nadezhda's sobs faded. Had she fainted from the stress? Too afraid to break eye contact with Vladimir, she dared not check.

"But you married Yuri anyway. I was patient. I waited. You made me do these things."

A step up for her, and another back for him.

He had almost reached the top. Behind him, she saw the man from the bar take a step down. She allowed herself to glance at him for only a moment. He caught her gaze and made a movement with his arms, signaling he planned to grab Vladimir.

"I didn't know how you felt," she said. "You should've told me."

Another step. He didn't match hers.

"I tried. That night in my apartment, but you left."

Her legs trembled with the next step. She was getting closer.

"It was too soon. I couldn't explain it to you then. I didn't understand it myself."

He stared past her, talking more to himself than to her. "I thought I finally had all I wanted, but you ran away. When I saw you with Ahmed and those other men, I knew I had to fight for you, or lose you again. I was the one who told them about the FSB. It almost cost me my deal."

She used the time to get closer.

"That's why you hid at the hospital."

"You knew that too?" he asked, staring at her. "But I used the time to save my deal. I got the money for you. For us. So we could be together."

The man from the bar was behind him now, only a step away. She stood on the stair just below him.

"I want that," she said, meeting his gaze. "To be with you."

She reached out her right arm and placed it around his neck. As she leaned forward to kiss him, her left arm dangled over the side of the staircase. Her fingers brushed Nadezhda's swinging leg.

He leaned forward and touched his lips to her, then grunted into her mouth. She closed her hand over Nadezhda's leg. In an instant, Vladimir was struggling in the other man's bear hug, and Nadezhda swung in her grip.

Out of nowhere, uniformed guards swarmed about them. One guard helped her pull the child up and over the rail. As soon as Nadezhda was in her mother's arms, she wailed again.

The rest of the guards surrounded the two struggling men and pulled Vladimir back, pinning his arms to his sides. Only then did she realize she'd been wrong about the man from the bar.

Descending to where she comforted her daughter, the big man asked in an accented voice, "Is she all right?" Still out of breath, she could only nod in response. "Name's Marcus Gordon. Sergei sent me."

"Sergei's alive? But you're not — you're American."

"Criminals aren't the only ones who operate internationally." He jutted his chin toward Vladimir. "Does he still have the virus?"

When she glanced in Vladimir's direction, he thrashed about in the guards' grasp. "You bitch. You stupid bitch. You've ruined everything."

"When he left me, I think he gave it to Ahmed."

"Ah, yes. Ahmed. We'll be able to see him from here."

He nodded to one of the guards and spoke into a radio. Following Gordon's gaze, she watched three security guards run up the gangway of another plane.

A few minutes later, they appeared, escorting Ahmed between them. He shouted at them in broken Russian about being insulted, but stopped in mid-sentence when he saw Vladimir on the stairs. Before the agents with him could react, he reached into a duty-free gift bag and pulled out a teddy bear and held it over his head, shouting at them to let him go.

"My bear," Nadezhda said. "That man has my bear."

After exchanging glances, the agents stepped back, allowing Ahmed to back toward the plane's departure gate. At the gangway entrance, he turned to run onto the plane. With his back to the terminal, a shot thundered through the cavernous building. Ahmed fell and the entire departure hall exploded into screams and general confusion.

Marcus grabbed her arm and led her down the stairs. At the bottom, he picked up the things they'd left and escorted her toward the gate, talking quickly. "Get on the plane."

"But Vladimir…the virus — "

"I promised Sergei to help you. Get on that plane. It's your one chance. Run and don't look back. I'll take care of the FSB."

Nodding, she moved toward the gate, but stopped and turned. "Expose the virus to sunlight to kill it."

"Go," he said with a nod and handed her Vladimir's case and their other carry-ons.

Her legs trembling, she trotted to the gate. At the entrance, she glanced back over her shoulder. Two guards were leading Vladimir out of the departure hall.

She handed her boarding pass to the attendant still standing there.

"Was that your husband?" she asked, checking in Vladimir's direction.

"No."

"Good. My husband used to beat me. I wished someone would've arrested him." She broke off part of the ticket and handed back it to her. "Welcome aboard."

On the plane, Alexandra dropped into her seat and strapped Nadezhda into the seat beside her.

"Can't I sit in your lap?" Nadezhda asked.

"After the plane takes off."

"And you'll tell me stories?"

"Of course. I'll tell you lots of stories."

"But only happy stories. I don't want any scary ones right now."

She smoothed the hair back from her daughter's forehead. "I don't either."

"What are we going to do in Turkey?"

"I don't know. Go on holiday, I guess."

"Without Uncle Vladimir?"

"Yes."

"Good. He took my bear."

The plane engines roared, and they settled back into their seats as it moved away from the terminal. Once in the air, Alexandra took a deep breath and began, "A long time ago in a country far, far away…"

Despite her nap in the bar, Nadezhda soon dozed off again. Rearranging her daughter on the seat, Alexandra caught sight of

Vladimir's briefcase. Glancing up to check the flight attendants' locations, she determined they were busy in the galley, where the clink of glass and the aroma of heating food drifted into the cabin. With a pat on Nadezhda's head, she picked up the case and carried it to the bathroom.

Chapter Forty

Sergei scanned the crowd before him and spotted his quarry to the left, behind a group of foreigners. He stepped off the sidewalk, letting his bare feet sink into the warm sand. As usual, he felt out of place, but even more uncomfortable than normal in his wrinkled suit, his trouser cuffs rolled up above his ankles and barefoot. He sweated profusely in the Sri Lankan midday sun.

He'd only needed a few phone calls to track her down after Marcus had briefed him on what had transpired at the airport. And that's what concerned him. If he could find her, so could others.

Ignoring the odd looks from the others on the beach, he trudged through the sand to where she lay on a towel in the sun, eyes closed, skin glistening with oil. A surge of desire passed through him. Her bikini's few strips of cloth gave her a sexier air than if she were naked. Once he neared her, he saw the child curled up on another towel under an umbrella's shade.

When he cast a shadow over her face, she opened her eyes and squinted at him. "To quote an old Russian saying, you certainly aren't in your own plate."

He smiled. "I am bit overdressed, aren't I?"

She sat up and moved to one edge of the towel. Patting the free space next to her, she said, "Take off your jacket and enjoy the sun."

He dropped his shoes, and after carefully placing his jacket on an edge of the towel, eased down next to her.

"I heard they shot you," she said, glancing at the sling over his arm. She turned and watched the waves crash against the shore. "Vladimir told me you were dead. When he said that, I felt as if the floor had disappeared beneath me."

"According to Marcus, you managed very well on your own."

She faced him, and a grin flitted across her lips. "I was hardly on my own. Thank you for sending Marcus…and the guards."

"I read the reports. You were the one who figured it all out."

"He had Nadezhda. I wasn't going to let him hurt her."

"A mother's love. He should've never tested that."

She glanced behind her at the child. "I feel as if it's been tested more than I could endure this past year."

"What are your plans now?"

"I'm working on visas for Europe. It's amazing how easy it is to get things when you have enough money."

"Two million dollars is a lot of money."

"How did you know — "

"Marcus. Vladimir kept mumbling about it all the way to the station. I'm afraid he's not a very brave man. He's provided enough information to arrest a number of people as well as deport a few more."

"I saw the stories in the foreign papers they sell here. I hope you got some credit for breaking an international bioterrorism ring."

"Some. Of course, my supervisor Yevgeny made sure it was his name in the papers."

"Yes, I do recall that name."

"Sometimes you have to accept you did what was right and not worry about who receives the credit."

"I appreciate my name not appearing."

"That's why I'm here," he said, his voice growing grave. "You can be certain the Iranians aren't happy. They didn't get the virus, a scientist for their program, or the money they paid out. If I could find you here, so can others."

She dug her toes into the sand. "I know. I have enough money to buy new documents, but I'm afraid I'm not good at this. There's no sign advertising 'False Identities Sold Here.'"

"Perhaps I can help." He reached over to his jacket and handed her a large envelope from its inside pocket.

"My name is now Elena Petrovskaya?" she asked, studying one of the passports it held inside. "You do a very good job making it appear old and used."

"Did you know the CIA did a very good job of making Russian passports too — except the staples they used didn't rust and Russian ones did. You learn a lot of interesting trivia when you work with the CIA. They're very grateful as well. Check inside."

Stopping at one page, she glanced up in surprise. "American visas?"

"If you choose to live there, they'll be glad to arrange for permanent residence. America is a big country. You could get quite lost there, especially with two million dollars."

"Not to mention arranging for Nadezhda's operation."

"What if — " He glanced over at the sleeping child and cleared his throat. "What if the operation doesn't work? Have you ever thought about that?"

She stared down at her feet, now buried up to her ankles in the sand. "All the time. But at least I'll know I've done everything I could for her. When I helped you, it was for her, to keep her safe."

"Speaking of keeping her safe. I've spoken with your friend Lena. I would suggest you not contact — "

"I know it was wrong of me, but I just had to talk to her one last time. To let her know why I wouldn't be calling again. It's going to be very lonely."

"True, but I can tell you from experience you can get used to it."

"You prefer being alone?"

"I don't know if I *prefer* it, but compared to some other choices — like living with someone who resents the fact that you care about your work over making a name for yourself — it's certainly more peaceful."

"You care about your job?"

"My ex-wife said too much."

"Not interested in giving it up?"

He glanced at the waves, choosing his words slowly. "It wouldn't work, Sasha. It's not that I don't care about you, but — "

"There's something you care about more." She shook her head. "I can't compete against a whole country."

"Maybe there's still a way for me to help you out."

He stood and offered her his hand. After she rose, he waved to his travel companions, and couldn't suppress a smile when she squealed. "Katerina? Ivan? How?"

"Russia is no longer safe for them either. And as you said, it's a very lonely existence, even with two million dollars."

He wasn't sure she heard all of his explanation. She'd run to Yuri's parents to embrace them.

Leaning down to pick up his shoes, he gave one last glance at Nadezhda, her hope. Blowing a kiss in the child's direction, he watched her stir slightly in her sleep. Without calling to Alexandra or the others, he sauntered past them and toward the street.

Acknowledgments

This story's inception involved two elements: a copy of Richard Preston's March 9, 1998 *New Yorker* article "Annals of Warfare: The Bioweaponeers," and my work in Russia. I didn't work in the area of bioweapons or even with the military, but I did work in the field of healthcare and was familiar with the state of the Russian medical field following the fall of the Soviet Union. As I continued my research for this novel, two books provided additional insights into the development of bioweapons in the US and Soviet Union: *Biohazard* by Ken Alibek and Stephen Handelman; and *Virus Hunter* by C.J. Peters and Mark Olshaker. I began this story while still living in Russia, and would like to acknowledge the reality checks provided by my friends and colleagues Lara Petrossyan and Kami Rhabani. I also received support from my neighbors and colleagues at USAID/Moscow, the Rosinka complex, and all my fellow writers in the following chapters of Romance Writers of America: Dallas Area Romance Authors, Elements, the Golden Network, and the Pixie Chicks. This novel has gone through several drafts, and has only grown in strength from the comments and advice of various contest judges, including Paula G. Paul from the Southwest Writers; my creative writing teachers Dr. Nancy Jones Castilla and Richard Abshire; and my special critique partner, Vicki Batman. Finally, support from my family has been vital, and I want to thank my husband, Raul, and my children, Raul, Roberto, and Fernanda, for seeing me through the various stages of creation and revisions.

About the Author

Liese Sherwood-Fabre grew up in Dallas, Texas and knew she was destined to write when she got an A+ in the second grade for her story about Dick, Jane, and Sally's ruined picnic. After obtaining her PhD from Indiana University, she joined the federal government and had the opportunity to work and live internationally for more than fifteen years. After returning to the states, she seriously pursued her writing career and has had numerous pieces published. You can follow her upcoming releases and other events by joining her newsletter. When you subscribe, you will also get a free download of short story available only to those who sign up at her Website:

Website: http://www.liesesherwoodfabre.com

Or you can visit:

Facebook: https://www.facebook.com/liese.sherwoodfabre/

Twitter: @lsfabre

Email: liese@liesesherwoodfabre.com

Other Books by Liese Sherwood-Fabre

CURIOUS INCIDENTS: MORE IMPROBABLE ADVENTURES

Welcome back to Baker Street! Holmes and Watson are there to greet you once more with amazing tales of murder, mayhem, and mystery with a supernatural twist. This time the great detective and his stalwart companion will venture into alternate universes, histories, and futures to solve puzzling cases of the paranormal beyond the bounds of imagination.

THE LIFE AND TIMES OF SHERLOCK HOLMES: ESSAYS ON VICTORIAN ENGLAND

Step back to 1895 England.

Sir Arthur Conan Doyle's stories are full of references to everyday Victorian activities and events that send the twenty-first century reader to consult a reference book. Few, for example, are intimately acquainted with the responsibilities of a country squire, the importance of gentlemen's clubs, or the intricacies of the Victorian monetary system.

CORAZONES

A collection of three award-winning literary short stories exploring the impact of love. "A Stranger in the Village," nominated for the 2007 Pushcart Prize, describes how the arrival of a young woman into a Mexican mountain village changed sixteen-year-old Hector forever. "Sacrifice" offers an Aztec tale of political intrigue and love. In "Curandera," Doña Rosa assists the lovelorn through the heartache of passion and infidelity.